TIME CHANGES

stories and recipes from *jovi's* kitchen

Cooked up by Jonnie Anderson and Vivian Jones

The Paper Journey Press
Wake Forest, North Carolina

Time Changes
stories and recipes from jovi's kitchen

©2008 The Paper Journey Press
The Paper Journey Press
an Imprint of Sojourner Publishing, Inc.
Wake Forest, NC USA

The Paper Journey Press: http://thepaper journey.com
First trade paperback edition
Manufactured in the United States of America

 Library of Congress Control Number: 2008936897

International Standard Book Number (ISBN) 0977315681

Cover photo by Greg Allen
Cover design by Dan Russell
Artist rendering of *jovi's cafe* on back cover by Eric Keravuori

Special thanks to *A Toast to the Triangle* for use of logo.
Special thanks to *Raleigh: The Magazine of the Triangle* for use of photo.
Special thanks to *The Wake Weekly* for use of previously published photos.
Special thanks to *The Herald Sun* for use of photo of newspaper.

TIME CHANGES

stories and recipes from *jovi's* kitchen

We dedicate this book to all of our family and friends who made this journey possible …

And a word to Jane and Delette—this is the way we remembered it and we are sticking to it!

Jonnie & Vivian

Chapter One

A Restaurant is Born

Some people paint; others knit or write to express their creativity, Jonnie and I cook.

Looking back, we realize we were being taught by example. We grew up in a rural setting with a garden and livestock. Our mother was a homemaker with five children and a husband who was gone a lot with his job. She ran the house, planted and harvested the garden, grew beautiful flowers, fed the children, sewed our clothes, helped out in the community, and still managed to have a great meal on the table at the end of the day.

Jonnie and I didn't plan to cook for a living when we were kids. I dreamed of being a housewife like my own Mother. Jonnie, the baby of the family, was a fabulous organizer and excellent with numbers.

In 1981, my former husband and I had moved to Wake Forest so that he could attend the seminary. Somewhere along the way, I found myself working at Variety Wholesalers, divorced, with a daughter in Wake Forest-Rolesville High School and a son at North Carolina State University. Jonnie was Assistant Vice President of Operations for First National Bank of Randolph County in Asheboro. Both of us wanted

Recipes from jovi's were often featured in local and regional newspapers and magazines. These days Vivian frequently finds herself in the spotlight as Wake Forest's first female Mayor.

to make changes in our lives; since we loved to cook and entertain, we decided to start a restaurant. Never mind the fact that neither of us had ever worked in a restaurant.So in the middle of our lives, we changed course. *No pun intended.*

Sisterhood to business partners—scary! But we made it work. Jonnie moved to Wake Forest in 1991 where the two of us spent the next nine months making *jovi's* a reality.

The name jovi's is a combination of the first two letters of our names, which was a suggestion of my good friend Chris Harper. We each had definite ideas about the kind of restaurant we had in mind. We wanted a place that was quiet and comfortable where our patrons would feel like they were guests in our homes rather than customers. Our goal was to create a restaurant where people could relax, enjoy a good meal and feel at home.

jovi's PIMIENTO CHEESE

- 24 oz. Grated SHARP Cheddar cheese
- 3/4 cup pimiento, drained
- 2-1/2 Tablespoons cider vinegar
- 1/4 teaspoon salt
- 1/2 teaspoon pepper
- 1/2 cup mayonnaise

Puree pimiento in blender or food processor until smooth. Mix all ingredients and chill. You may want to add a little more mayonnaise. Some people like more than we do. Please use real mayonnaise!

Jonnie Anderson and Vivian Jones

Originally, we had considered the building on North White Street that now houses *The Cotton Company*. We liked the location, but as we explored upfitting soon realized it was just too large for our first venture.

Meanwhile our friend, Barbara Lyon called and asked, "Have you thought about our little house on Jones Avenue?" After taking a look, we thought the size and charm of the old house fit. The home's simple, gracious lines with its rocking chair front porch reflected our desire to keep it simple. *The house was perfect. In a word, we were sold.*

Stuffy was not in our vocabulary.
We wanted nice. Gracious. Elegant. But not snooty.

Nine months after we began our preparations, *jovi's* was ready to host its first customer. Not wanting to make a mistake our first official day of business, we decided to host a practice dinner inviting many of our friends to attend. This gave our wait staff and cooks an opportunity to go through all the steps before we actually had paying customers. Neither cash nor credit would be needed for this event. All we asked was that they pay for their meal by "filling out a comment card."

We were thrilled when our friends, Doug and Sally Jurney planned to come all the way from Rocky Mount to attend. Things at the restaurant went well throughout the evening. But we wondered why Doug and Sally were so late. We found out when they walked through the door cold and somewhat strident. As they were making their way to Wake Forest on Highway 96, driving through the country east of Bunn, a deer jumped into their car. Sally said she suddenly had a deer head in her lap!

Bless their hearts; they still drove up to Wake Forest despite a broken window and freezing temperatures. Doug's classic Jaguar spent several days in the shop. He never lets me forget that my invitation for a free dinner was the most expensive he's ever eaten!

Stories just happened at *jovi's*. It wasn't enough for us to serve a meal. We wanted our food and service to reflect our efforts to please the palate more than creating a cutting-edge culinary experience. We preferred to provide our customers with good service and delicious food. We found our pleasure in serving.

Our customers became our friends. And our friends became our customers.

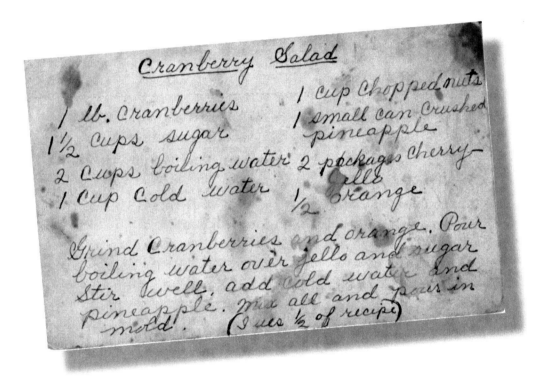

We cherish this well-worn and much utilized handwritten recipe from Mother's recipe box. This card was given to her by Mrs. Currie when we were children. We are so thankful that she set it down on paper for Mother.

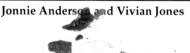

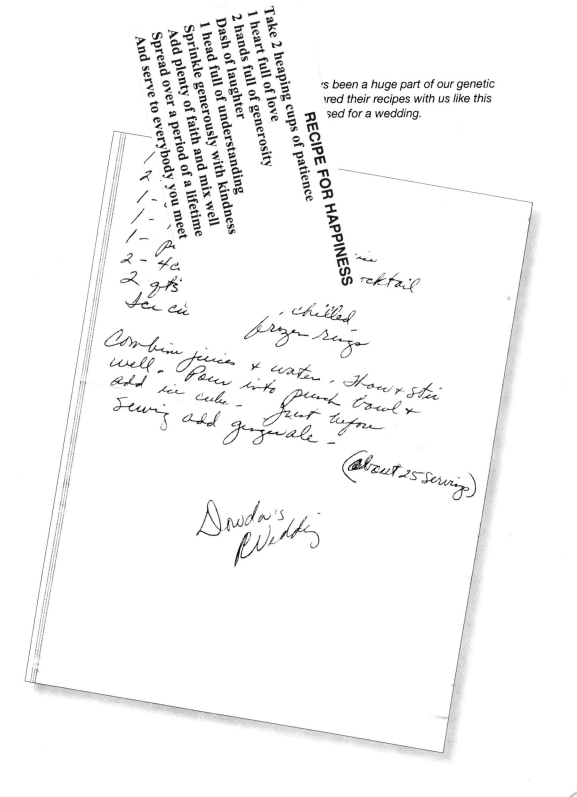

...s been a huge part of our genetic
...red their recipes with us like this
...sed for a wedding.

RECIPE FOR HAPPINESS

Take 2 heaping cups of patience
1 heart full of love
1 hands full of generosity
2 hands full of laughter
Dash of understanding
1 head full of understanding
Sprinkle generously with kindness
Add plenty of faith and mix well
Spread over a period of a lifetime
And serve to everybody you meet

...cktail

chilled
frozen rings

Combine juices + water, show + stir
well. Pour into punch bowl +
add ice cube. Just before
serving add gingerale –

(about 25 serving)

Drida's
R Wedding

Chapter Two

The Backstory

Without a doubt our mother is our muse in the kitchen. We grew up in Randolph County, North Carolina, with two older sisters and an older brother. Our father worked for a commercial flooring contractor. A perfectionist who took great pride in his work, Daddy laid wood floors and tiled hundreds of businesses and offices all over the Southeast but especially in North Carolina including the floors of the new Wake Forest University at Winston-Salem.

Until I moved to Wake Forest, I was unaware of the disappointment that accompanied the moving of Wake Forest College to Winston Salem. For our family that move had been a pretty good deal because my father and his crew laid all of the floors in the University buildings there. Since it took over a year to complete, Daddy was home every night instead of working off somewhere.

Mother took care of the home front as a housewife and doting mother. Daddy's work often took him away for days at a time, but she didn't let this get her down. Mother was good at stretching our budget. She took great pride in our surroundings, tending the yard as well as the house. The yard was always beautiful with flowers, shrubs, and trees.

Mother holding Vivian outside our home in rural Randolph County. Mother's energy and enthusiasm for life inspired the five of us to work hard.

Despite having five children and a husband who traveled, Mother found the time to maintain a large vegetable garden. A wonderful cook, the garden provided a good source of wonderful meals cooked and enjoyed by relatives and neighbors alike. Mother worked hard and she expected us to help her as we grew up. As we became teenagers, she would give us the job of cooking dinner while she worked in her beautiful flower beds.

Since Daddy expected biscuits at every meal, Mama made them so often she did not need a recipe. In order for me to learn to make the biscuits, I would put flour in the bowl and take it with some shortening to Mama working in the flower beds to make sure I had the correct amounts. When I got married my husband was very excited that I could make homemade biscuits. *The trouble was that I could only make 15 — no more, no less — that's what fit in Mama's pan!*

Here's Jonnie during her "bathing beauty" days!

jovi's Tiny Little Biscuits

- 1-1/2 cup self-rising flour

- 1 cup whipping cream

Mix flour and cream gently only until well blended. Butter hands very well with soft butter and form dough into small balls. You will need to butter your hands after every 2 or 3 biscuits. Place on baking sheet 1" apart. Bake in 425° oven for 10-12 minutes until just beginning to brown.

At the restaurant, *jovi's little biscuits* became one of the most popular items we served! Guests loved them and usually wanted more than one basket.

Our loyal customer, Mr. Weisskopf was called the "biscuit man" because he could eat at least two dozen by himself!

The hostess would alert the kitchen when he came in so we could put another pan of biscuits in the oven! You can make them ping-pong ball size, but we usually made them small because we thought it was unique and they were so easy to pop into your mouth!

Our loyal customer, Mr. Weisskopf, was called the "biscuit man" because he could eat two dozen by himself!

You can successfully double or triple the recipe. We actually made four times the recipe, rolled them out, put them on a paper-lined cookie sheet and froze them. After the biscuits were frozen, we put them in a plastic bag taking out a pan full at a time to cook. You do not have to thaw. Put them in the oven frozen. *Simple, fast, and delicious!*

Chapter Three

A Family Affair

Everyone in our family pitches in to help when there's something to do. So it was inevitable that our family would be a big part of jovi's. Mother and Daddy financed us. Our brother Steve and brother-in-law Henry did all of the necessary remodeling of the house. Our niece Dianne came and helped us get ready including re-upholstering chairs. She stayed and worked with us for several months—as long as she could stand it.

Our sisters, Jane and Delette came and helped us at the HerbFest every year. Once our niece Amy also came. Jane would come down and help us cater the Southeastern Baptist Theological Seminary (SEBTS) Trustee luncheon every year. She made such good apple pie that they always asked " is Jane coming to help?"

Mother made all our dresses for sister Delette's wedding. Jonnie is in the foreground eyeing the beautiful homemade-wedding cake.

Jane and Vivian are the real cooks in our family. I follow recipes very well, but I don't have the innate artistry that they seem to bring to the kitchen. Delette is very talented in many ways but only cooks when she has to. Generally she schedules her life in such a way that she doesn't get caught in the kitchen very often. Cooking is not her thing. She has Mama's other talent—working with her hands in crafts and art.

Daddy had a great way of making his point that family should be together for the holidays!

Our mother sewed all of our clothes when we were little. I think we can all remember the first store bought garment we had. Mine was a Chesterfield coat . . . boy did I feel special. Looking back I am amazed that Mama did what she did. All four girls would have a new outfit to wear for Easter and Christmas. We would go to church in our new

BERRIED TREASURE

This was a favorite dessert at jovi's. We usually filled a dish with sliced fresh strawberries, spooned on the topping, and sprinkled with a little brown sugar. You can also use blueberries, raspberries, peaches, or some combination of all of them.

TOPPING:

- 6 ounces cream cheese, softened

- 8 ounces sour cream

- 1/3 cup light brown sugar, packed

Beat cream cheese until smooth. Add sour cream and brown sugar and beat until smooth. Chill thoroughly.

outfit and then come home to a wonderful meal, often with company invited. Mama had somehow done it all.

After Daddy retired at age 70, he would dye Easter eggs every year—and still does. He would write each of his children's names on an egg with a pencil before he dyed them. One year, I chose to go to the beach with friends at Easter—the first time I had ever missed being home for Easter. I went by to see Mama and Daddy before leaving and there was no egg with my name on it.

"Daddy, you forgot me?" I asked. He replied, "No, if you're not here, you don't get an egg."

I have never made that mistake again.

Daddy is known for the chickens he doodles on church bulletins. Actually, we believe this is the only thing he can draw. Before our church used bulletins, he would grab the hand closest to him and one of us would leave church with a chicken on our hand.

Time Changes: stories and recipes from *jovi's* kitchen

Chapter Four

Stirring the Pot

Our Mama and her sister Gerry began making Brunswick stew together more than 50 years ago. They made it on Saturday after Thanksgiving and made enough for both of them to freeze containers for their family to eat during the winter. After a few years, they began inviting siblings and families to join them for a Brunswick stew dinner. This was a way to have a mini family reunion in the fall. For us, "mini" was a relative term since my mother had thirteen siblings. Sometimes we would have as many as eighty people gathered in our backyard as Mother and Aunt Gerry stirred sixty-three gallons of stew in a big, black pot outside on a wood fire.

After Mama died, we stopped hosting the big family get-together with our aunt, but Daddy still must have his Brunswick stew. We now combine his annual birthday party with our stew-making. Besides, from a practical standpoint, making a big pot of stew is easier than having a luncheon since we have a time getting him to keep his guest list

Vivian and Jonnie visiting with some of the cousins.

below 100! The stew is a family affair with nieces and nephews helping out, and it has also become a community affair.

Standing around stirring the pot with family and friends is one of my favorite parts of the day. Using the corn and tomatoes from Daddy's garden that had been "put up" during the summer brings the whole day full circle.

Another tradition we have is pecan cookies at Christmas. Mama only made these cookies at Christmas, so the anticipation for them was always great. Her cookies were the best. We all make them but no one can make them quite as good as Mama. The first year Jane's daughter Debbie was going to be away from home for Christmas, Jane called her and told her she was sending her some pecan cookies. Debbie said, "That's great, Mom, But can you send some of Grandmother's?"

For our family get-togethers, "mini" was a relative term since my mother had thirteen siblings.

We have concluded that Mama's were the best because she used fresh pecans that she shelled and sliced with a paring knife rather than the automated chopping most of us engage in now. Since her special care and patience did not crush the oil out of the pecans, they were more flavorful.

Nowadays, if we don't have at least 20 to 25 people for a family meal we don't know what to do. We seldom have a meal without extra neighbors, friends or extended family present. This is the tradition that Mama and Daddy started years ago. Even after we all got married, we always felt that we could invite our friends to those special meals. Now our kids sometimes bring their friends.

Traditions are important to our family—most of them involving food. Dianne says that we will use any excuse to get the family together. *We hope some of our recipes will inspire you to start a tradition in your own family.*

BRUNSWICK STEW

- 4 pounds beef (like sirloin tip)

- 4 pounds pork (loin)

- 3 large stewing hens

- 1-1/2 pounds carrots quartered and sliced

- 1-1/2 pounds onions diced

- 3 quarts butterbeans (fresh or frozen)

- 12 quarts tomato juice

- 3 quarts corn (fresh or frozen)

- 10 pounds potatoes peeled and diced about ½ inch size

- 1 head cabbage

- 2 or 3 pods red hot pepper

- ½ pound butter

Boil beef, pork, and hens in separate pots in salted water until very tender. Remove from heat and chop up removing all bones, skin, and fat. Save broth to use in stew.

Place potatoes in pot with water to cover. Bring to a rolling boil, add butterbeans, reduce heat, and cook until tender, about 20 minutes. Add carrots, broth, and juice gradually, keeping the mixture simmering at all times. Add onions and corn. Continue cooking for 15 to 20 minutes. Add meat gradually, keeping the mixture simmering. Add cabbage and butter. We add the hot peppers now and leave them in for 15 minutes or so and then take them out. We do not like for the stew to be too hot. Also, salt and pepper a little as you add the ingredients.

Taste toward the end to see if you need more. Continue to simmer for 30 minutes or so. You should stir frequently and once the meat has been added, you will need to stir gently continuously. This will make about 30 quarts or so. If it is too thick, just add more juice or a little water. If it is too thin, continue to cook until it thickens up.

Chapter Five

Taking Stock

We grew up with the example that you tried to make your community a better place and helped your neighbors. When we started jovi's we made a commitment to each other that we would be involved in downtown and in the total community.

Mother and Daddy taught us early on the importance of giving back to our community. Mother was always involved in the PTA. She was a member of the Home Extension Club. I can remember going to meetings with her when I was small. The women learned gardening, crafts, cooking, and homemaking.

I also remember going with mother to my aunt

Daddy has a variety of interests. This photo was taken when he was a young man. These Shetland ponies are pulling a sled.

and my grandmother's homes where women in the community gathered to work on quilts. The quilts would be sold at auctions to raise money for the church or they simply helped each other make quilts for their own use. I can remember playing under the quilting frame and sometimes the ladies asking me to thread needles for the older women who had trouble seeing.

Daddy was on the local school board for a number of years and he served on the board of directors of the local volunteer fire department when it was started. I believe I was a teenager when they formed the fire department. Daddy was the treasurer at Bethel Methodist Church for years. He finally gave up the job when he turned 91.

Mother could make the most simple of meals like her Turnip Greens and Cornbread seem elegant.

Early on, Jonnie began working in the Wake Forest Downtown Revitalization Corporation (DRC). She served a term on the Wake Forest Chamber Board, serving as Chair in 1997-1998. Rejoining the DRC in the early 2000s she served on the board of directors until recently. She has remained an active volunteer with the DRC and Chamber of Commerce for more than fifteen years.

Since I was the chief cook/chef at *jovi's*, it was more difficult for me to get away but I did manage to serve on the DRC for a couple of years. When we closed the restaurant portion of *jovi's*, I was elected to the Town Board and two years later was elected as the first female Mayor of Wake Forest. Since then I have spent my time working at that job! I could not have done my job without Jonnie's help.

Jonnie took over when I had to be at meetings and events and never complained — well almost never!

TURNIP GREENS

Lisa McCamy told me I had to put this recipe in the book. As you will see, I really don't have a step-by-step quantity recipe. We just always cooked however much we had available!

So here goes, if you have trouble or questions, give me a call. Thoroughly wash your greens. I always wash them in hot water — my mother said that would make varmints turn loose and float to the top! I usually wash them 3 or 4 times to be sure the sand/dirt is gone.

Place the greens in boiling, salted water. You can cook a whole bunch at a time because when you put them in the water they will wilt immediately. Bring them back to a boil and simmer them for a couple of hours. Yes, a couple of hours!

Remove from the water and drain. Chop the greens — I don't like them chopped too small but that's your choice. Next sauté the greens in a little oil (we used to use fatback or bacon grease but that's not politically correct these days) for 15 minutes or so — on medium heat. You don't want to brown them, just incorporate the flavor of the oil. Salt and pepper to taste. Serve with a little vinegar and don't forget the cornbread!

CORNBREAD FOR FOUR

This is a simple recipe that will make an 8 or 9 inch cast iron frying pan full

- 1/4 cup flour
- 3/4 cup plain cornmeal
- 2 teaspoons baking powder
- 1/2 teaspoon salt
- 1-1/2 tablespoons solid shortening
- 1 egg
- 3/4 cup milk
- 1-1/2 tablespoons solid shortening for pan

Put the shortening in the pan and place in hot oven while you mix the batter. Mix dry ingredients, cut in 1-1/2 tablespoon shortening, add egg and milk. Mix lightly. Pour batter into hot pan and bake 15-20 minutes at 450°.

NOTE: *you may use self-rising cornmeal and omit the baking powder and salt. 3 times the recipe makes 2 dozen regular size muffins.*

Chapter Six

Good Corporate Citizens

We always tried to be good business citizens and participate in events happening in the area. For several years we were a part of **A Toast To The Triangle,** a fund-raising event for *The Tammy Lynn Center*. The first year we did the Toast, we were a little nervous since we had never done anything like that. Here we were, a little upstart business in Wake Forest bringing in our simple one vase of flowers, one chafing dish, and two silver trays to set up on one table … and they had put us between *Sisters Catering*, a famous Raleigh caterer and *The Angus Barn*!

The *Sisters* had a huge display with a live mermaid and *The Angus Barn's* space was four tables long with barrels of their signature cheese and six foot tall racks of pies!!

I turned to Vivian and said, "Why were we invited to do this?" But, the aroma of Vivian cooking mini crab cakes on site soon drew a crowd and our bite size meringues filled with chocolate mousse and lemon curd were declared the best dessert in the house. We gave of our time, food,

IN APPRECIATION OF
YOUR PARTICIPATION

A Toast To
The Triangle™

1996

and money whenever we could to help organizations in town. We always laughed when people would ask for a donation and say it was tax deductible. That didn't mean a lot to us since you have to make money for a tax deduction to be important!

We had great fun catering the Mardi Gras Ball several years. They were held in interesting places back then-once in the old cotton warehouse that later became The Cotton Company. There was no electricity, water, etc. The Cultural Arts Association had to string up lights for the occasion! It was also held once in the Keith's Grocery Store building (now The Forks Cafeteria) and in the old Lyon's Grocery Store. When you have volunteers putting together a fun evening and everyone expecting to have a great time, you don't need a fancy place! At the request of the Cultural Arts Association, we set up a hotdog table the first year of the concert series. We have enjoyed personally and professionally being a part of our community.

Living downtown is a treat. One of our hopes is that more owners will turn their upper stories into condos.

In 1995 we became true "downtowners" in every way when we rented the second floor of the Wake Forest Frame Shop building from John and Barbara Lyon. We have a great apartment with tall ceilings, big rooms, and lots of history. More history was made in 1996 when Hurricane Fran came roaring through Wake Forest in the middle of the night. Being downtown, we did not have to worry about trees falling on us but we had a swimming pool on the rooftop! The wind blew off the cover that channeled water to the downspouts. That water had to go somewhere and it poured down the walls of our apartment. Even the next day when the sun came out we still had water pouring! My Dad called to see if we were okay and wanted to know if we were washing dishes because he could hear it over the phone.

Jonnie Anderson and Vivian Jones

CRAB CAKES

- 1 pound fresh crab meat
- 2 slices very dry bread crumbs
- 2 oz. Sautéed-in-butter finely diced onion
- 2 Tablespoons softened butter
- 1-1/2 teaspoon dry mustard
- 1/8 teaspoon pepper
- 1 egg

Mix all ingredients together and form into cakes.
Saute slowly in butter until very brown.

John worked valiantly with several roofing companies but it took six to eight months to get the roof completely fixed. In the meantime, we just piled our furniture in the middle of the floor. Eventually we got a new wall and a paint job. We never regretted being in the apartment even when we were eating supper at a card table in the bedroom.

We love living downtown; one of our hopes for downtown is that other property owners will turn their upper stories into apartments or condos. Local architect Matt Hale has successfully melded loft living on the upper floors and office space on the ground floors in his building. His building has brought us great neighbors.

One thing about being downtown that came as a big surprise to me was being awakened by birds singing on our windowsills. They roost on our bedroom windows. We had lived in the country for forty years and never had that problem.

Jonnie now travels once a week to look after Daddy for a few days. He is now 95, but still sharp as a tack; and he still grows the best tomatoes. He is very happy when Jonnie makes pancakes with whipped cream for breakfast or chicken and mashed potatoes for supper like Mama did during their sixty-four years of marriage.

This is the guest register from our 5th Anniversary Open House. We were pleased and proud of the attendance and cherish the sweet comments people wrote.

Chapter Seven

Little Kitchen, Big Customer Service

We had a tiny kitchen in jovi's. It is amazing to look back and realize how much we were able to do in that small space.

Our former chef Mark Carroll said he loved working at jovi's because of the butt rubbing! We usually had two cooks and a dishwasher with wait staff coming in and out all the time. We never actually dished the plates until the wait staff told us a table was ready. Then we would get them out as quickly as possible. Needless to say, tempers sometimes flared; Vivian was known for having a short fuse at times. Everyone tiptoed around when that happened. But most of the time we had plenty of fun. On slow nights all the employees would gather in the back discussing and solving world problems.

Speaking of Mark Carroll, he and his wife came for dinner one night. He began telling Jonnie that he was getting ready to enroll at

Our galant chef Mark Carroll was a gifted cook. When we found out he was going to culinary school we asked him to work for us right on the spot.

Wake Tech in their culinary arts program. We practically hired him on the spot. He worked for us during his entire tenure at Wake Tech. Mark helped us with our first catering job. After he completed the program, he left and went to work at a larger restaurant to get more experiences. From time to time, he came back and helped with catering jobs. In fact, just about two years ago he helped us with our last one.

Having your own business is too hard if you can't feel good about something at the end of the day.

We wanted our guests to have a pleasant, comfortable visit to our restaurant just as we had always entertained visitors to our home. The wait staff never rushed someone through a meal just so we could "turn a table". I always tried to have the wait staff be as attentive as the customer wanted or needed them to be to fit the occasion.

We served a lot of customers who became friends and we talked with them in that way. Sometimes they would come in with another couple or a business colleague, and you would need to give them their privacy. A good waitperson knows the difference. A lot of business people go out to lunch to have a conversation with a customer or co-worker, not with the wait staff. I had some businessmen compliment me that the staff did not constantly interrupt them asking questions like "Do you want more tea?" Our staff would just pour more if your glass was empty. We insisted that the staff knew if you were drinking sweet or unsweetened, regular or decaf so they did not have to interrupt to give you refills.

Another thing I insisted on was they clear and clean the table before they asked for a dessert order. Presentation is part of enjoying a meal and what dessert isn't better on a clean table. If you aren't sitting there looking at a dirty plate, dessert becomes a special part of the meal. Sometimes you don't even realize little things that have made a meal more enjoyable. When the customer leaves the table, the only things left at the table should be their beverage glasses or cups and their napkins.

ROAST PORK LOIN WITH PEPPERCORN CRUST

- Boneless pork loin (5-6 pound)
- Crushed black peppercorns
- 4 green onions
- 1/4 cup wine (red or white)
- 1 tablespoon of flour
- 1 cup beef broth

Press peppercorns into roast on all sides. Place in roasting pan and roast at 325° for approximately 30 minutes per pound or until internal temperature reaches 160.

In skillet pour drippings from roast (no more than 1/2 cup). Sauté finely chopped onion for 30 seconds. Add a tablespoon of flour and whisk until smooth. Add wine and cook uncovered for 1 minute. Add beef broth and simmer for 2-3 minutes. Serve sauce over slices of roast.

One thing the wait staff teased me about was serving hot coffee. The area where we kept coffee cups in the back tended to be cold, so in the winter the porcelain coffee cups would be cold enough to make the coffee lose heat. We kept a pot of hot water to fill the coffee cups to preheat them, dump out the water, and then pour the coffee. We were constantly getting compliments on our good coffee.

I realize my ideas are out-dated. I was raised before kids were entertained during the meal with television, etc. The family talked to each other during a meal. I remember the adults sitting around the table for a long time with their coffee just visiting. We have been trained by restaurants to think the hurried, noisy atmosphere is the way to have a meal.

In this hectic atmosphere, some restaurants can "turn the table" seating more people during the night to increase the bottom line. For me, this does not translate into a good experience. When I go out with friends for dinner, I want good food and a pleasant conversation in a relaxing atmosphere. You should not have to shout over the music or the folks at the next table. And you should not be rushed through your meal.

One couple obviously didn't subscribe to my philosophy. They arrived around 7:30 one particularly rainy and messy evening and said "We had planned to go out for dinner tonight, but didn't want to drive to Raleigh in the weather!" I was amused that they did not consider our place as going out for dinner. Happily for both of us, they were not forced to eat at our place too often!

Maybe we would have been more financially successful if we had used those tactics, but we measure our success by the number of wonderful friends and relationships we have made. The memories we have sometimes make us laugh and sometimes make us cry. But we did the things the way we felt comfortable, and I think that is important.

Having your own business is too hard if you can't feel good about something at the end of the day.

Chapter Eight

Entertaining with Grace and a Good Sense of Humor

Our niece, Dianne Murphy, came and worked with us. We never would have been able to open the doors without her! She had worked for large restaurant management companies. She was the only one of the three of us who knew what we were doing! A few months after we were open, she called her mother, our sister Jane, and told her that she was worried about us. Dianne couldn't understand our business model. "They think they are entertaining people in their home," we heard her telling her mom on the phone.

On our first day, we opened for lunch. After we

had served our first guest, Dianne, who was serving as hostess, came into the kitchen and announced that we had not stocked the cash register!! I quickly wrote a check and Spencer took off for the bank to get change.

*Family was the key to jovi's success. Here, Vivian's daughter, Wendy, serves up some fun and delicious food at **A Toast to the Triangle**.*

When the first customer requested a "to-go" order, of course, we were not prepared. No plastic or paper. They wanted a salad, so we put it in one of our glass bowls, wrapped it in cling wrap and told them to bring it back the next time they came!

We were lucky to have great employees who were always willing to go the extra mile. One day, Kevin, one of the wait staff went flying out the back door in the middle of lunch without a word to anyone. We were extremely perplexed because he was currently serving tables.

In just a few moments he was back. A customer had requested a straw but we had forgotten to stock them. Kevin ran out the back door

CRANBERRY SALAD

- 1 pound cranberries, ground in food processor
- 1-1/2 cup sugar
- 1 cup chopped pecans
- 1 – 10 oz. Can crushed pineapple
- 2 cups boiling water
- 1 cup cold water
- 2 – 3 oz. Packages cherry Jello
- One fresh orange

Grate zest from orange, then peel and mash up the pulp of the orange

Dissolve Jello in boiling water. Add cold water. Mix all ingredients, pour into bowl and chill overnight or until firm.

*(**Note:** You can make this sugar free by using sugar-free Jello, Splenda, and no-sugar-added pineapple. We always make some this way for a couple of friends who have diabetes.)*

across the lot to Hardee's and took a few until we could get our own supply. Always try to please the customer. Thanks, Hardee's!

Our right-hand man, Spencer Hubbard, was responsible most of the time for delivering lunches that we catered off site. We did a lot of catering at Circuit Board Assemblers (later bought out by Flextronics) in Franklin County. One day for their Board of Directors meeting, we had prepared a luncheon of Chicken Pie with a couple of sides which included our Mother's Cranberry Salad. This was a favorite with our guests.

Even corporate executives were required to try a little bit of everything at jovi's!

When one of the board members served himself from the buffet, he asked what the salad was in a rude manner. Spencer told him that it was our cranberry salad. The board member said, "Well, I don't want any of that." Spencer replied, "You have to try a little of everything. It's a rule before you can have dessert." The president of CBA was chagrined because he was afraid this usually brusque and blunt board member would be unkind to Spencer. However, the board member simply nodded and said, "Okay." Later the man went back and got some more! The president really enjoyed telling us about the exchange. He said we could send Spencer to his office anytime!

No party was too small or too far away for us. We catered a lot for the larger local industries, usually carrying food to their facilities for business luncheons. We also catered for many smaller businesses and social functions from Louisburg to Cary.

Chapter Nine

Secret's In the Soup

When we meet our former customers on the street, some of their fondest food memories involve our soups.

One of the favorite soups we made was our semi-famous Crab Soup. Everyone said it was the best they ever ate. Now I have to admit that the recipe is not some gourmet extravaganza. In fact, it is made with cream of celery soup!

Another customer favorite was our potato soup that we made from our Mother's recipe.

When we were young and suffering an "upset tummy," Mother would make potato soup for us. Of course, she would not add onions since this was medicinal!! We loved this soup even if it was medicine, so I'm sure we had "upset tummy" more than necessary.

One day we had Potato Soup as our lunch Soup of The Day, and Dr. Harvey from SEBTS commented, "I like Potato

Soup with onions, have you ever tried it?" I, of course, replied, "My mother never put onions in her potato soup!" After that, Dr. Harvey

always asked if a dish was one of my Mother's recipes before he made any suggestions. Perhaps it had been the tone of my voice that day because many times after that I would hear him warning others not to comment on anything if I had said it was "cooked by her mother's recipe."

CRAB SOUP

- 50 oz. Cream of celery soup
- 2 teaspoons Old Bay Seafood Seasoning
- 2 teaspoons Worcestershire sauce
- 1 teaspoon garlic salt
- 1 teaspoon pepper
- 1 cup melted butter
- Mix all together until smooth. Gradually add:
- 1 cup heavy cream
- 7-8 cups milk
- 4 boiled eggs, chopped

Heat until boiling. Add 1 pound crab meat. Stir constantly until crab meat is hot. Serve.

Makes 4-5 quarts

Chapter Ten

Just Desserts

Everyone makes German Chocolate Cake, but I always thought my mother's was the best. Of course!

Finally, I realized the difference! The difference between her recipe and others is that when making the frosting she added the coconut and pecans along with all the other ingredients and cooked them all together. Other recipes call for them to be added after you remove the pan from the heat. This is the secret. The pecans and coconut have a better flavor when they are cooked instead of raw.

I realized her change was **probably because she could dump every**thing into the pot at once and her daughter who loved this cake and was constantly asking for it could then stir the icing while it cooked. As you know this is a time consuming process. Mother could then get other things done while the icing cooked. It also kept me out of trouble for a while.

We loved serving the most delicious desserts in town, but had a rule that we simply did not sing "Happy Birthday."

Time Changes: stories and recipes from *jovi's* kitchen

GERMAN CHOCOLATE CAKE

- 1 cup margarine
- 2-1/2 cups flour
- 2 cups sugar
- 4 eggs, separated
- 1 teaspoon baking soda dissolved in
  1 cups buttermilk
- One 8 oz. Package German Sweet Chocolate
  dissolved in 1/2 cup boiling water
- 1/4 teaspoon salt

Cream margarine and sugar until light and fluffy. Add egg yolks, beating well. Add flour alternately with milk. Add chocolate. Beat egg whites with salt until stiff but not dry. Gently fold egg whites into batter. Pour into 3 greased and floured cake pans and bake at 350° 25-30 minutes until tester comes out clean. Cool for 10 minutes, remove from pans, and cool completely before frosting.

Most restaurants sing "Happy Birthday" to customers, but not *jovi's*. No singing. Someone asked why we didn't and Vivian replied, "Because Jonnie might want to join us"! No one can be more honest to your face than a sister. I love music, but have no musical talent.

We loved our friends, but even they could not convince us to sing.

A group of friends who always came to jovi's to celebrate their birthdays together brought us a teddy bear that would sing "Happy Birthday" when you pressed its paw. From then on we could offer a little music for celebrations.

One evening Bill and Emily Andrews were having dinner with some friends. The Andrews were frequent guests at *jovi's*. They told

GERMAN CHOCOLATE FROSTING

- 2 cups sugar
- 1 15 oz. Can evaporated milk
- 1 cup chopped pecans
- 1 cup shredded coconut
- 3 egg yolks
- 1 stick butter
- 1 teaspoon vanilla

Put all ingredients in a saucepan, bring to boil, and cook slowly until thickened, about 20 minutes. Stir constantly. To test for doneness, put 3-4 drops on a saucer, turn sideways. If it doesn't run, then it is ready. Remove from heat, let cool. When cool, frost cake. We always frost between layers and around sides. Some people just put the frosting between the layers which is a lot easier but I don't think it looks as good!

Jonnie about a recent visit to Charleston, South Carolina where they had eaten in a fancy French restaurant. The chef and wait staff had sung operatic selections during the evening to entertain the guests. Bill and Emily were teasing Jonnie that jovi's needed to step up and provide that kind of engaging entertainment for out guests. Jonnie related the message to me. At her suggestion when things slowed down a bit in the kitchen, I went to the Andrews' table and sang, "I'm a little teapot, short and stout. Here is my handle, here is my spout, etc." with appropriate gestures and motions.

Needless to say, they never again mentioned the staff singing to them!

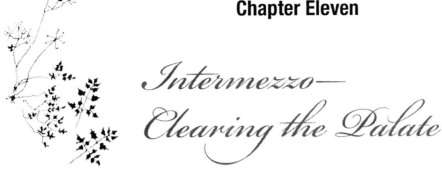

Chapter Eleven

Intermezzo— Clearing the Palate

In 1998, Jonnie and I were at a crossroads with the restaurant. We decided to close the restaurant and create jovi's market and catering. We focused on catering and desserts. The saddest part of our decision was giving up the "Special Dinners" that we staged seasonally at Valentines and New Years. Our friends kept coming by the store, but many of them repeatedly expressed regret at how much they would miss the "Special Dinners."

We loved creating these one-of-a-kind dinners. We would have an elegant, price-fixed menu with four or five courses and an Intermezzo of sorbet to clear the palate before serving the entrée. We had a great time preparing for these dinners. They enabled us to create some elegant entrees and other courses that we did not serve at other times.

Wake Forest engineer Eric Keravuori presented this pencil drawing to us after the fire department staged their controlled burn.

We actually tried lots of new things that we had never prepared before. We had a loyal following for our dinners. Recently one of my long-time friends told me that she had kept every one of our menus.

Valentine's Day guests were usually romantic twosomes. But on New Year's Eve, groups of people would come together. One year we had a group of twenty from Henderson. Our good friends from St. John's Episcopal Church came every year for the last seating of the night. We enjoyed visiting with them at the end of the evening when we could relax and maybe even have a hearty laugh at ourselves. People seemed to love the fact that they had the opportunity to wear fancy dresses and tuxedos in Wake Forest.

People loved the fact that they could wear fancy dresses and tuxedos during our "Special Dinners."

The year after we closed the restaurant, a good customer approached us. Her son was planning to propose to his future wife on New Years Eve and because of his fond memories of our "little" place, wanted us to set up a table in our shop and serve them dinner. Since we no longer had tables and chairs. we decided to invite them to our home! We set up a table in the corner of our living room in front of the window and served them dinner. Between courses, we would disappear to the back. It snowed that night and was beautiful with the candlelight and the snow!

Looking back, we achieved our goal of creating a business that nurtured friendships as much as the palate.

FRESH ORANGE SORBET

- 2-1/2 cups water
- 1 cup sugar
- Orange rind strips from 2 oranges
- 2-2/3 cups fresh orange juice
- 1/3 cup fresh lemon juice

Combine water and sugar in small saucepan and bring to a boil. Add orange strips and reduce heat. Simmer for about 5 minutes. Discard strips and let liquid cool completely.

Add orange juice and lemon juice. Pour mixture into a container and freeze.

Jonnie Anderson and Vivian Jones

Chapter Twelve

Time Changes

We have so many happy memories. This one is a perfect example of how you have to go with the flow as time or incidents dictate.

One fall we had a special Sunday Brunch scheduled for a family after the christening of their new baby. They were to arrive immediately after the 10 o'clock mass from the Catholic Church. This was when St. Catherine's of Siena was still in the old stone church on South Main Street now used for weddings and other events. We went in early that day and prepared a brunch of breakfast casserole, cheese strata, fruit and breads. We were promptly ready at 11 o'clock more than a little proud of our efforts to have everything ready for the group to arrive.

We waited. And waited some more.

Expecting them to arrive soon, we did what we could to keep the food warm. We became frustrated that we had to hold the food for so long. We had no idea what was keeping them. Our imagination ran wild — did the service run long or had they stiffed us to have brunch somewhere else? At 11:55 Jonnie decided to drive up to the church to see what was going on. As soon as she got there, folks began streaming out. She hurried back, soon followed by the group. We got everyone in — seated and served them though we were a little miffed that no one bothered to apologize for being late. They loved the food and left a very generous tip. Jonnie and I cleaned up and simply chalked it up to, "The customer is always right."

That evening Jonnie, my daughter Wendy, and I arrived at our good friends the Matheny's for dinner and board games. We arrived promptly at 6 p.m. — the appointed hour. We have known the Matheny's for a long time, and we were a little surprised when they seated us in their formal living room. We were even more surprised when our usually informal friend Durward served us drinks and then left us alone to drink them. We could hear Shirley bustling around in the kitchen, which was also very unusual because they are very organized and ready when guests arrive.

We arrived promptly at 6 p.m. and were a little surprised that our friends were not ready.

At some point Durward rescued us from the formal living room and the evening progressed. We were having a great time. Jonnie asked, "What time is it? I have to get up early tomorrow." Wendy looked at her watch and said, "Oh, goodness, it's midnight." Shirley looked at us a little dumfounded. "There's a clock on the wall and it's only 11 o'clock.

The three of us burst out laughing having realized that we had been an hour ahead all day because the time had changed. We had gained an hour but forgot to set our clocks back. Of course, we apologized to the Matheny's for our early arrival. They had gone with the flow as any good host would.

After closing the restaurant, we became jovi's kitchen and catering and concentrated on catering and desserts. That quickly evolved into an expanded menu of prepared foods, fully cooked, which we packaged into servings of two, four and ten. We froze these for the customer to heat at home. Like our original restaurant we didn't know what we were doing or even what to call this type of business since there were none around to copy. Did that stop us? Of course not! Sometimes ignorance is bliss. At one point, our friend Carole Caniford opened a little antique shop in our spare room. When she decided it was more fun to spend her weekends at the beach, we changed again. This time, we became jovi's kitchen and market. And again with a friend, Gayle Adams, we stocked specialty foods and kitchenwares.

Judy Berry and her son Max walked in one day just to check us out. We started talking and she said she had worked at a very similar place in Augusta. I told her we were looking for part time help if she was interested. She came in a day or two later, met Vivian, and we hired her on the spot. Judy made our last years at our shop easier and much more fun. She has always teased us saying she has never known anyone as trusting as we were. On her first day we gave her a key. We always started out by trusting our employees, then let them prove if they were

BARBECUED MEATBALLS

- 1-1/2 pounds ground beef
- 3/4 cup bread crumbs or cracker crumbs
- 1 cup milk
- 3 teaspoons minced onion
- 1-1/2 teaspoon pepper

Mix all ingredients and form into balls. Mix sauce recipe below.

- 3 tablespoons sugar
- 2 tablespoons Worcestershire sauce
- 1 cup ketchup
- 1/2 cup water
- 3 tablespoons cider vinegar
- 6 teaspoons minced onion

Pour sauce over meatballs and cook at 350° for an hour or so until well done. Chill and remove fat from top. Reheat to serve.

worth it or not. Very few times have we been disappointed.

When another change appeared on the horizon — our little building was going to make way for an exciting new downtown project — we tested the water by opening a booth at The Cotton Company. After several months, the sale was finalized and we moved entirely to The Cotton Company except for catering. At that point in our life, we decided we were too old to keep catering anyway — it's hard work — and we didn't want to go through the expense of upfitting another kitchen for health department approval. So as we watched our building go down in flames, literally, we went on to another venture.

MARINATED SHRIMP

- 1 pound peeled, cooked small or medium-sized shrimp
- 1/2 cup lemon juice
- Hot sauce (like Tabasco or Texas Pete) to taste
- 1/2 cup olive oil
- 3/4 cup white vinegar
- 1/4 cup honey
- 1 cup green olives with juice
- 1 medium sized purple or white onion, sliced thin

Salt to taste

Combine lemon juice, hot sauce, oil, vinegar, and honey and stir well. Add olives, onions, and shrimp and salt to taste. Stir gently. Cover and refrigerate 1 hour or overnight.

Jonnie and Vivian look on as their former restaurant is used for a control burn by the Wake Forest Fire Department.

Our booth at The Cotton Company is already changing. We recently added an Antiques and Collectibles section. This gives us a valid excuse to go to Hoy's Auction, which we love. People and businesses have to be willing to change to stay vibrant and interesting. But nothing pleases us more than for our old customers to seek us out at events or our new location and share their memories of what was.

Time's do change.

Come on In!

Appetizers
&
Hors d'oeuvres

jovi's PIMIENTO CHEESE

24 oz. Grated SHARP Cheddar cheese

3/4 cup pimiento, drained

2-1/2 Tablespoons cider vinegar

1/4 teaspoon salt

1/2 teaspoon pepper

1/2 cup mayonnaise

Puree pimiento in blender or food processor until smooth. Mix all ingredients and chill. You may want to add a little more mayonnaise. Some people like more than we do. Please use real mayonnaise!

jovi's CHEESE SPREAD

1/2 pound grated sharp Cheddar cheese

1/2 pound softened cream cheese

1 teaspoon garlic salt

1 teaspoon dry mustard

2 Tablespoons Worcestershire sauce (1/4 cup)

2 Tablespoons Tarragon Vinegar (1/4 cup)

Stale beer (up to 1/4 cup)

Paprika

Mix all ingredients with enough beer to work and make soft. Chill until hard enough to shape into balls. Shape into two balls and roll in paprika.

Note: You can substitute cider vinegar but cut back to 1 Tablespoon. Also, you can use freshly opened beer but stale is better.

HOT CRAB DIP

8 ounces cream cheese, softened

4 tablespoons milk

1 tablespoon white wine

2 teaspoons Worcestershire sauce

1/3 teaspoon dill weed

2 tablespoons finely chopped green onion

8 ounces fresh crabmeat

In a small saucepan, combine first 5 ingredients and stir over medium low heat until melted. Stir in onion and crabmeat. Heat, stirring until hot and blended. Serve in chafing dish with crackers.

CRAB MOUSSE

6 ounce can tomato soup

4 ounces cream cheese

1/2 cup mayonnaise

2 teaspoons finely chopped onion

1/2 cup finely chopped celery

1 ounce unflavored gelatin softened in 1/4 cup cold water

6 to 8 ounces fresh crabmeat

Warm soup slowly. Add cheese and gelatin. Beat until smooth. Cool for a few minutes. Add remaining ingredients. Place in mold or bowl and chill until set.

Time Changes: stories and recipes from *jovi's* kitchen

SUN-DRIED TOMATO AND CHEESE SPREAD

7 ounces sun-dried tomatoes in olive oil

8 ounces cream cheese softened

1/2 cup grated Parmesan cheese

1/2 cup butter softened

1 tablespoon chopped fresh basil (or 1/2 tablespoon dried)

1/2 teaspoon dried thyme

Drain tomatoes, reserving 2 tablespoons of oil. Set aside 1/4 cup tomatoes. Reserve remaining tomatoes in oil for another use. In food processor with knife blade, place 1/4 cup tomatoes, 2 tablespoons oil, cream cheese, and remaining ingredients. Pulse until well blended. Chill thoroughly. Let come to room temperature to serve. Serve with crackers.

MARINATED SHRIMP

1 pound peeled, cooked small or medium-sized shrimp

1/2 cup lemon juice

Hot sauce (like Tabasco or Texas Pete) to taste

1/2 cup olive oil

3/4 cup white vinegar

1/4 cup honey

1 cup green olives with juice

1 medium sized purple or white onion, sliced thin

Salt to taste

Combine lemon juice, hot sauce, oil, vinegar, and honey and stir well. Add olives, onions, and shrimp and salt to taste. Stir gently. Cover and refrigerate 1 hour or overnight.

BARBECUED MEATBALLS

1-1/2 pounds ground beef

3/4 cup bread crumbs or cracker crumbs

1 cup milk

3 teaspoons minced onion

1-1/2 teaspoon pepper

Mix all ingredients and form into balls. Mix sauce recipe below.

3 tablespoons sugar

2 tablespoons Worcestershire sauce

1 cup ketchup

1/2 cup water

3 tablespoons cider vinegar

6 teaspoons minced onion

Pour sauce over meatballs and cook at 350° for an hour or so until well done. Chill and remove fat from top. Reheat to serve.

SHRIMP MOUSSE

1 envelope unflavored gelatin dissolved in 1/4 cup cold water

1 can tomato soup

8 ounces cream cheese

1/2 cup mayonnaise

1/2 cup whipped cream

1/2 cup chopped green olives

1 tablespoon grated onion

1 tablespoon butter

Salt to taste

1 tablespoon hot sauce (like Tabasco or Texas Pete)

1 tablespoon Worcestershire sauce

1 cup finely chopped green pepper

1/2 cup finely chopped celery

1 pound chopped boiled shrimp

Heat soup in double boiler. Add cheese, onion, and butter. Stir until smooth. Add gelatin and cool. Add mayonnaise, whipped cream and other ingredients. Turn into mold or bowl and refrigerate for 2 hours or overnight

BOURSIN CHEESE SPREAD

8 ounces softened butter

16 ounces cream cheese softened

2 cloves garlic, pressed

1/2 teaspoon oregano

1/4 teaspoon each, basil, dill weed, marjoram, black pepper, and thyme

Mix all ingredients thoroughly in mixer or food processor. Refrigerate overnight to blend flavors. Serve at room temperature with crackers. May be frozen. This is delicious on hamburgers, turkey sandwiches, etc.

MARINATED EYE OF ROUND

4 pound eye of round roast

1 cup soy sauce

1/4 to 1/2 cup gin

1/2 cup vegetable oil

4 crushed garlic cloves

Trim fat from roast and place in a ziplock bag. In a bowl combine remaining ingredients. Pour into bag with roast. Close bag and refrigerate for 48 hours, turning roast several times. Preheat oven to 500. Pat roast dry and bake for 20 minutes. Turn oven off and wait 20 minutes. Remove from oven, wrap in foil, and refrigerate several hours or overnight. Slice very thin and serve with Horseradish Sauce and rolls.

Horseradish Sauce

1 cup heavy cream

1 cup mayonnaise

pinch salt

1/4 to 1/2 cup prepared horseradish, or to taste

Whip cream until soft peaks form. Beat in mayonnaise and salt. Stir in horseradish.

NOTE: You can also cook a beef tenderloin this way. Cook it for about 45 minutes.

BLACK BEAN SALSA

1 cup canned black beans, rinsed

1 cup fresh diced tomatoes

1/2 cup whole kernel corn

4 green onions sliced

Fresh cilantro

1/2 teaspoon cumin

2 tablespoons orange juice

Salt to taste

Hot sauce (such as Tabasco or Texas Pete)

Mix beans, tomatoes, corn, and onions. Mix 2 to 3 teaspoons minced cilantro, cumin, salt, and orange juice. Add a couple dashes of hot sauce. Mix well. Serve with tortilla chips.

4 cans black beans, drained and rinsed

1 large onion, chopped

6 gloves garlic, minced

1 3-inch piece of ginger root, chopped

3 tablespoons butter or oil

1 cup sour cream

6 eggs

2 teaspoons salt

1 tablespoon pepper

Spring Onion Sauce (see below)

1/2 red bell pepper and 1/2 green bell pepper, cut into very thin strips

16 ounces feta cheese, crumbled

Saute onion, garlic, and ginger in butter until soft. Set aside to cool. Pulse beans in food processor until coarsely chopped. (You can do this by hand, but it is harder!) In a large bowl, mix beans and onion mixture. Add sour cream, eggs, salt and pepper. Mix until well blended. Place mixture in buttered loaf pan or tureen. Cover with buttered foil. Place loaf pan in larger baking pan and fill with enough hot water to come halfway up the sides of loaf pan. Bake at 350° for 1 hour and 15 minutes or until firm. Cool completely. Put on plate and top with Spring Onion Sauce. Sprinkle pepper slices and feta cheese all over. Serve with crackers.

SPRING ONION SAUCE

1/2 cup red wine vinegar

2 tablespoons Dijon style mustard

2 spring onions, including green tops

3 cloves garlic

1 teaspoon sugar

1-1/2 cups olive oil

Salt and pepper to taste

In food processor, combine vinegar, mustard, onions, garlic, and sugar. Process until well blended. With machine running, add olive oil in a SLOW, STEADY stream. Season with salt and pepper. Refrigerate. This will keep for quite a while in the refrigerator.

HERB SEASONED POPCORN

1 (3.5 ounce) package butter-flavored microwave popcorn

1/2 teaspoon dried basil

1/2 teaspoon dried thyme

1/2 teaspoon dried parsley

6 ounces mixed canned nuts

Prepare popcorn according to package directions. Carefully open bag and add herbs to popcorn. Close bag and shake. Pour into container. Add nuts and toss gently.

SHRIMP SPREAD

4-5 ounces cooked shrimp, chopped finely

1/2 cup finely chopped celery

1 green onion with top, finely chopped

12 pimiento-stuffed green olives, finely chopped

1 hard-boiled egg, chopped finely

1 teaspoon lemon juice

dash pepper

1/4 cup plus 1 tablespoon mayonnaise

Combine all ingredients. Serve with crackers or croutons.

HERBED CHEESE TARTS

Vegetable Pan Spray

1/3 cup fine dry bread crumbs

8 ounces cream cheese softened

3/4 cup cream-style cottage cheese

1/2 cup shredded Swiss cheese

1 tablespoon all purpose flour

1/4 teaspoon dried basil

1/2 teaspoon garlic powder

2 eggs

Sour cream

Sliced black olives

Spray 24 muffin cups with pan spray. Sprinkle bread crumbs onto bottoms and sides of cups to coat. Set aside.

Combine cream cheese, cottage cheese, Swiss cheese, flour, basil, and garlic powder in mixer and beat on medium just until fluffy. Add eggs and beat on low speed just until combined. Fill each muffin cup with cheese mixture and bake at 375° for 15 minutes or until set. Tarts will puff while baking and will deflate as they cool. Cool for 10 minutes then remove from pans. Cool thoroughly. To serve, put a dollop of sour cream on top and one or two slices of black olive. You can also put a dollop of red caviar on top instead of the black olives.

These may be made the day before. Simply refrigerate and add the sour cream and olives just before serving.

MAMA'S CHEESE BALL

My mother always made this cheese ball for the holidays.

8 ounces cream cheese

1 pound grated cheddar cheese

4 ounces blue cheese

1/2 cup mayonnaise

1/2 cup sherry

1 teaspoon salt

1 tablespoon hot sauce (like Tabasco or Texas Pete)

Finely chopped pecans

Mix all ingredients except pecans and form into two balls. Roll in chopped pecans. Refrigerate. Serve with crackers.

Salads
and
Vegetables

MOTHER'S CRANBERRY SALAD

1 pound cranberries, ground in food processor

1-1/2 cup sugar

1 cup chopped pecans

1 – 10 oz. Can crushed pineapple

2 cups boiling water

1 cup cold water

2 – 3 oz. Packages cherry Jello

1 fresh orange – grate zest from orange, then peel and mash up the pulp of the orange

Dissolve Jello in boiling water. Add cold water. Mix all ingredients, pour into bowl and chill overnight or until firm.

(Note: You can make this sugar free by using sugar-free Jello, Splenda, and no-sugar-added pineapple. We always make some this way for a couple of friends who have diabetes.)

BLUE CHEESE DRESSING

1/2 cup sour cream

2 Tablespoons mayonnaise

1 Tablespoon lemon juice

Tops of 2 green onions, chopped

3/4 cup crumbled blue cheese (4 oz.)

1/2 teaspoon Worcestershire sauce

Combine all ingredients and mix well.

BRAISED PEAS WITH DILL

2 – 10 oz. Boxes frozen green peas

1 large red onion, diced

1/4 cup olive oil

2-1/2 cups water

2 Tablespoons chopped dill

Salt and pepper

Heat oil in large saucepan. Add the onion and cook over moderate heat, stirring occasionally, until softened but not browned. Add the other ingredients. Bring to a boil and then simmer over moderate heat until the water has evaporated and the peas are very tender, about 30 minutes. Serve hot.

LEMON GLAZED CARROTS

1 pound carrots, peeled

2 Tablespoons butter

Juice and grated rind of 1 lemon

2 Tablespoons sugar

Salt and pepper to taste

Slice carrots into rounds or strips. Cook carrots in boiling water for about 8 minutes. Drain. Combine butter, juice, and rind in pan and sauté carrots. Sprinkle with sugar, salt and pepper. Cook over medium high heat until glazed.

CRISPY HALF BAKES

2 large baking potatoes

2 teaspoons melted butter

1 teaspoon lemon juice

2 Tablespoons grated Parmesan cheese

Pepper to taste

Cut potatoes in half lengthwise. Brush cut surfaces with a mixture of butter and lemon juice. Dip cut side of potato halves into mixture of Parmesan and pepper to generously coat. Place cut side down on well greased baking pan. Bake at 375° for 30 minutes or until potatoes are tender. Using a thin spatula, turn potatoes right side up immediately to prevent them from sticking to the pan.

SHREDDED YAM CASSEROLE

2 pounds raw sweet potatoes

1 cup sugar

1/2 cup light corn syrup

1/2 cup water

1/4 cup butter

1   8 oz. Can crushed pineapple

Grated nutmeg

Fill large pot with salted cold water. Peel and shred raw potatoes and drop immediately into salted water. Combine sugar, syrup, and water. Bring to a boil and boil for five minutes. Remove from heat. Add butter and stir until melted. Drain potatoes and place in a 13x9 casserole dish. Pour pineapple over potatoes and then pour sugar syrup over. Sprinkle grated nutmeg on top. Bake uncovered at 350° for approximately 1 hour or until potatoes are transparent.

(Note: You may add a lattice crust to the top. It looks pretty and tastes delicious!) Serves 10.

TURNIP GREENS

My good friend, Lisa McCamy told me I had to put this recipe in the book. As you will see, I really don't have a step-by-step quantity recipe. We just always cooked however much we had available! So here goes, if you have trouble or questions, give me a call.

Fresh Turnip Greens

Oil

Salt and Pepper to Taste

Thoroughly wash your greens. I always wash them in hot water—my mother said that would make varmints turn loose and float to the top! I usually wash them 3 or 4 times to be sure the sand/dirt is gone.

Place the greens in boiling, salted water. You can cook a whole bunch at a time because when you put them in the water they will wilt immediately. Bring them back to a boil and simmer them for a couple of hours. Yes, a couple of hours!

Remove from the water and drain. Chop the greens—I don't like them chopped too small but that's your choice. Next sauté the greens in a little oil (we used to use fatback or bacon grease but that's not politically correct these days) for 15 minutes or so—on medium heat. You don't want to brown them, just incorporate the flavor of the oil. Salt and pepper to taste. Serve with a little vinegar and don't forget the cornbread!

Soups
&
Breads

CRAB SOUP

50 oz. Cream of celery soup

2 teaspoons Old Bay Seafood Seasoning

2 teaspoons Worcestershire sauce

1 teaspoon garlic salt

1 teaspoon pepper

1 cup melted butter

Mix all together until smooth. Gradually add:

1 cup heavy cream

7-8 cups milk

4 boiled eggs, chopped

Heat until boiling. Add 1 pound crab meat. Stir constantly until crab meat is hot. Serve. Makes 4-5 quarts

CREAMY TOMATO SOUP

3/8 cup minced onion

3-1/2 Tablespoons flour

4-1/2 Tablespoons margarine or butter

1 teaspoon salt

1/2 teaspoon pepper

1-1/2 cups milk

1 (46 oz.) can tomato juice

2 bay leaves

Saute onion in margarine in large saucepan until tender. Add flour, salt, and pepper, stirring until smooth. Cook 1 minute stirring constantly. Gradually add milk and tomato juice. Add bay leaves. Cook over medium heat until very hot and beginning to thicken. Remove bay leaves. Makes about 2 quarts.

POTATO SOUP

4 cups diced potatoes

4 cups water

1 teaspoon salt

½ teaspoon pepper

3 cups milk

1 cup heavy cream

¼ cup butter

2 tablespoons flour

Place potatoes, water, butter, salt, and pepper in pot and bring to a boil. Reduce heat and simmer until potatoes are cooked. Dissolve flour in water to make runny paste. Add to hot mixture and cook 1 minute. Add milk and cream. Heat until very hot. Serve.

Note: If you want to add onion, add them at the beginning. You may want to adjust seasonings to taste.

BRUNSWICK STEW

4 pounds beef (like sirloin tip)

4 pounds pork (loin)

3 large stewing hens

1-1/2 pounds carrots quartered and sliced

1-1/2 pounds onions diced

3 quarts butterbeans (fresh or frozen)

12 quarts tomato juice

3 quarts corn (fresh or frozen)

10 pounds potatoes peeled and diced about ½ inch size

1 head cabbage

2 or 3 pods red hot pepper

½ pound butter

Boil beef, pork, and hens in separate pots in salted water until very tender. Remove from heat and chop up removing all bones, skin, and fat. Save broth to use in stew.

Place potatoes in pot with water to cover. Bring to a rolling boil, add butterbeans, reduce heat, and cook until tender, about 20 minutes. Add carrots, broth, and juice gradually, keeping the mixture simmering at all times. Add onions and corn. Continue cooking for 15 to 20 minutes. Add meat gradually, keeping the mixture simmering. Add cabbage and butter. We add the hot peppers now and leave them in for 15 minutes or so and then take them out. We do not like for the stew to be too hot. Also, salt and pepper a little as you add the ingredients. Taste toward the end to see if you need more. Continue to simmer for 30 minutes or so. You should stir frequently and once the meat has been added, you will need to stir gently continuously. This will make about 30 quarts or so. If it is too thick, just add more juice or a little water. If it is too thin, continue to cook until it thickens up.

jovi's TINY LITTLE BISCUITS

One of the most popular things we served! Guests usually wanted another basketful of biscuits. We called Mr. Weisskopf the "biscuit man" because he could eat at least two dozen by himself! The hostess would alert the kitchen when he came in so we could put another pan of biscuits in the oven! You can make them ping-pong ball size, but we usually made them small because we thought it was unique and they were so easy to pop into your mouth!

1-1/2 cup self-rising flour

1 cup whipping cream

Gently mix flour and cream only until well blended. Butter hands very well with soft butter and form dough into small balls. You will need to butter your hands after every 2 or 3 biscuits. Place on baking sheet 1" apart. Bake in 425° oven for 10-12 minutes until just beginning to brown.

You can successfully double or triple the recipe. We actually made 4 times the recipe at a time, rolled them out, put on a paper-lined cookie sheet and froze them. When frozen, we put them in a plastic bag and would take out a pan full at a time to cook. You can put into the oven from the frozen state. Simple, fast, and delicious!

IRISH SODA BREAD

This was a recipe we used a few times to serve with our lunch special. Roe O'Donnell who is from Ireland told me it was pretty good!

2-1/2 cups all-purpose flour

1/2 cup sugar

1-1/2 teaspoons baking powder

3/4 teaspoon salt

1/2 teaspoon baking soda

1/2 cup butter

1 cup raisins

1 large egg

1-1/4 cup buttermilk

1/4 cup sour cream

Sift together the dry ingredients. Using a food processor or pastry cutter, cut the butter into the flour mixture until it resembles small peas. Blend in the raisins. Beat the egg, buttermilk, and sour cream together until blended. Stir the egg mixture into the dry mixture just until blended. Pour the batter into a 9 inch round cake pan that has been buttered well. Bake at 350° for about 50-55 minutes until a tester comes out clean.

Remove from pan and cool on a rack.

SHORTCAKE BISCUITS

These make wonderful cakes for strawberry or blueberry shortcake.

1-3/4 cup all-purpose flour

2-1/2 teaspoons baking powder

1/2 teaspoon salt

1 tablespoon sugar

1/4 cup butter

3/4 cup heavy cream

Sift flour, baking powder, salt, and sugar. Cut in butter to make coarse mixture. Add cream and stir lightly using a fork. Turn dough onto a lightly floured board and knead lightly for 30 seconds. Pat to 1/4 to 1/2 inch thick. Cut with a biscuit cutter and bake on a greased pan for 10-15 minutes at 450°.

LEMON NUT BREAD

1-1/2 cups flour

1/2 teaspoon salt

1 teaspoon baking powder

1/2 cup butter, softened

1 cup sugar

2 eggs, slightly beaten

1/2 cup milk

1/2 cup chopped pecans

Grated rind of 1 lemon

GLAZE: 1/4 cup sugar

Juice of 1 lemon

Mix together while bread is cooking

Sift flour, salt, and baking powder; set aside. Cream butter and sugar; beat in eggs. Add dry ingredients alternately with milk. Beat until smooth. Stir in pecans and lemon rind. Pour into greased loaf pan. Bake at 350° for 50 minutes or until done. Prick hot bread with a toothpick all over the top. Pour glaze on top of bread. Let stand 15-20 minutes. Remove from pan and cool completely before slicing.

CRANBERRY ORANGE BREAD

1 orange

1 egg, beaten

1 cup sugar

2 tablespoons butter

1/4 teaspoon salt

2 cups all-purpose flour

1-1/2 teaspoons baking powder

1 cup fresh cranberries, chopped coarse

1 cup chopped pecans

Grate rind of orange and squeeze juice. Add enough boiling water to the juice and rind to make 3/4 cup of liquid. Cream butter, sugar, and egg. Mix together the flour, salt, and baking powder and add to the egg mixture alternately with the liquid. Mix well. Fold in the cranberries and pecans. Spoon batter into greased and floured loaf pan. Bake at 325° for 45 to 60 minutes until tester inserted in middle comes out clean. Cool in the pan for 15 minutes.

ZUCCHINI BREAD

3 eggs

1 cup oil

2 cups sugar

2 cups grated zucchini

1 tablespoon vanilla

3 cups flour

2 teaspoons cinnamon

1/4 teaspoon baking powder

1 teaspoon salt

1 teaspoon baking soda

1 cup chopped pecans

Beat eggs until light and fluffy. Add oil, sugar, zucchini, and vanilla. Mix well. Mix together all the dry ingredients and add to the batter. Stir in pecans. Pour into TWO greased and floured loaf pans. Bake at 325° for 1 hour or more until tester inserted in middle comes out clean. Cool for a few minutes, remove from pan.

CORNBREAD FOR FOUR

This is a simple recipe that will make an 8 or 9 inch cast iron frying pan full

1/4 cup flour

3/4 cup plain cornmeal

2 teaspoons baking powder

1/2 teaspoon salt

1-1/2 tablespoons solid shortening

1 egg

3/4 cup milk

1-1/2 tablespoons solid shortening for pan

Put the shortening in the pan and place in hot oven while you mix the batter. Mix dry ingredients, cut in 1-1/2 tablespoon shortening, add egg and milk. Mix lightly. Pour batter into hot pan and bake 15-20 minutes at 450°.

NOTE: you may use self-rising cornmeal and omit the baking powder and salt. 3 times the recipe makes 2 dozen regular size muffins.

Entrées

We served this entrée at one of our New Year's Eve dinners

1-1/2 cups dried apricots

1/2 cup chopped pecans

1 clove garlic

1/2 teaspoon salt

1/2 teaspoon pepper

2 tablespoons dried thyme, divided

1/4 cup molasses, divided

1/4 cup vegetable oil, divided

1 (5 pound) boneless pork loin

1 cup bourbon

1 cup chicken broth

1/4 cup heavy cream

1/4 teaspoon salt

With knife blade in food processor, add first five ingredients. Process until coarsely chopped. Add 1 tablespoon thyme, 2 tablespoon molasses, and 2 tablespoons oil; process until mixture is finely chopped but not smooth.

Trim excess fat from pork loin. Make a lengthwise cut down the center of the loin, cutting to, but not through the bottom. Starting from center cut, slice horizontally toward one side, stopping about 1/2 inch from edge. Repeat on the other side. Unfold meat so that it is flat. Flatten the meat to 1 inch thickness using a meat mallet or rolling pin.

Spread the apricot mixture evenly on top of pork. Roll the loin, jelly roll fashion, starting with the long side. Secure the loin with string and place, seam side down, in a shallow roasting pan. Brush with 2 tablespoons oil, 2 tablespoons molasses, and sprinkle with remaining thyme.

Jonnie Anderson and Vivian Jones

Bring bourbon, chicken broth, and remaining 3 tablespoons molasses to a boil in a large saucepan. Remove from heat. Carefully ignite the bourbon mixture with a long match. Allow to burn until flames die. Pour over pork roast.

Bake at 350° for 1 to 1-1/2 hours or until meat thermometer registers 160°. Remove pork from pan, reserving drippings and keep warm.

Add cream and salt to pan drippings. Cook over medium-high heat, stirring constantly, until slightly thickened. Slice pork and serve with sauce.

NOTE: The bourbon must be burned off completely on the stovetop before baking to prevent bourbon from flaming in the oven.

MEATLOAF

3 slices day old bread, crumbled

1-1/2 cups milk

2-1/2 pounds ground beef

1/3 cup finely diced onion

3 eggs, well beaten

1-1/2 teaspoons salt

Combine crumbled bread and milk in large bowl and let sit for a few minutes. Add remaining ingredients and mix very well. Place mixture in loaf pan, making a slight indentation on the top. Spread sauce over and bake at 350° approximately 45 minutes.

SAUCE:

1/2 cup brown sugar

1 Tablespoon dry mustard

2/3 cup catsup

Combine all ingredients very well

SHEPHERD'S PIE

2-1/2 pounds ground beef, cooked and drained

1 cup chopped onion

2-1/2 teaspoons dried basil

2-1/2 teaspoons dried parsley

1-1/2 teaspoons dried thyme

27 ounces canned diced tomatoes

Creamed potatoes (approximately 3 large potatoes will make enough for this recipe)

Grated Cheddar Cheese

Combine all ingredients in large pot and simmer about 15 minutes. Place meat mixture in 13x9 baking pan. Cover with creamed potatoes. Sprinkle with grated cheese. Bake at 400° until bubbly and beginning to brown, approximately 25 minutes.

LASAGNA with GROUND BEEF

1-3/4 pounds ground beef

1/2 cup diced onion

1 large clove garlic

1-1/2 teaspoons salt

1 Tablespoon olive oil

1 teaspoon black pepper

1/2 teaspoon oregano

1/2 teaspoon basil

1 Tablespoon parsley

40 oz canned diced tomatoes

16 oz. Ricotta cheese

8 oz. Shredded Swiss Cheese

4 oz. Grated Parmesan Cheese

Uncooked Lasagna Noodles

1 cup water

Brown ground beef and drain off fat. Add next 9 ingredients and cook, stirring occasionally, for approximately 30 minutes.

Layer in 13x9 pan as follows: Just a little sauce, uncooked noodles, ½ of the Ricotta cheese, ½ of the Swiss cheese, ½ of the sauce. Repeat the layers. Sprinkle top with Parmesan cheese and a little basil. Pour water around edges of pan.

Bake at 350° for approximately 30 minutes.

ROAST PORK LOIN WITH PEPPERCORN CRUST

Boneless pork loin (5-6 pound)
Crushed black peppercorns

4 green onions

1 tablespoon flour

1/4 cup wine (red or white)

1 cup beef broth

Press peppercorns into roast on all sides. Place in roasting pan and roast at 325° for approximately 30 minutes per pound or until internal temperature reaches 160°.

In skillet pour drippings from roast (no more than 1/2 cup). Sauté finely chopped onion for 30 seconds. Add a tablespoon of flour and whisk until smooth. Add wine and cook uncovered for 1 minute. Add beef broth and simmer for 2-3 minutes. Serve sauce over slices of roast.

BLACKBERRY CHICKEN

SAUCE:

1/2 cup light brown sugar

1/2 cup seedless blackberry preserves

1-1/2 Tablespoons crushed garlic

1/3 cup white wine vinegar

1-1/2 Tablespoons olive oil

1 teaspoon ground cumin

Mix all ingredients together until smooth. This will keep in the refrigerator a long time

SPICE MIXTURE:

1-1/2 Tablespoons dried thyme

1 teaspoon paprika

1/2 teaspoon salt

1/4 teaspoon pepper

Mix together and keep in a covered jar

Choose baking pan to fit number of chicken breasts you want to cook. Cover bottom of pan with red wine. Place boneless, skinless chicken breasts in pan. Sprinkle heavily with spice mixture above. Spoon two to three tablespoons of sauce over each breast. Bake at 350° approximately 30 minutes or longer depending on number of chicken breasts. You may add fresh or frozen blackberries for the last 15 minutes of baking.

CHICKEN CHEDDAR BAKE

3 cups diced chicken

3/4 cup diced celery

2-3 oz. shredded Cheddar Cheese

1 cup Mayonnaise

1 oz. Almonds (sliced or slivered)

1/8 cup diced onion

1 Tablespoon lemon juice

Combine all ingredients, place in 13x9 baking pan and bake at 350° for approximately 20 minutes.

(Note: you may sprinkle the top with buttered cracker crumbs before baking)

CHICKEN PIE

1 (3 pound) stewing chicken

1 (14-1/2 oz.) can cream of chicken soup

1-1/4 cup chicken broth

1/2 cup (1 stick) margarine, melted

1 teaspoon salt

1/2 teaspoon pepper

1 cup self-rising flour

1 cup buttermilk

Boil chicken in water until tender. Reserve broth and remove chicken to cool. Skin and bone chicken and chop into bite-size pieces. Place chicken in the bottom of a large casserole dish. Set aside. In a medium bowl, mix together cream of chicken soup, chicken broth. Pour over chicken. In a medium bowl, mix together the margarine, salt, pepper, flour, and buttermilk. Whisk until smooth. Pour over chicken.

Bake in preheated 425° oven for 30 minutes or until browned on top and bubbly.

SOUR CREAM CHICKEN

3-1/2 cups diced cooked chicken

1 (14-1/2 oz.) can cream of chicken soup

8 oz. Sour cream

1 sleeve crushed Ritz or Saltine crackers

2 Tablespoons melted butter

Mix together the chicken, cream of chicken soup, and sour cream. Pour into baking dish. Mix butter and crackers and sprinkle over chicken.

Bake at 350° for approximately 30 minutes until hot and bubbly and crackers are beginning to brown.

DEVILED SEAFOOD

1/2 cup finely chopped green pepper

1/2 cup finely chopped onion

1/2 cup finely chopped celery

1 teaspoon Worcestershire sauce

1/2 teaspoon salt

1 (8 ounce) package cooked shrimp chopped

8 ounces fresh crab meat

2 cups herb seasoned stuffing

1 cup mayonnaise

Stir together all ingredients until blended. Spoon into shallow casserole dish and bake at 350° for about 30 minutes until beginning to brown around edges.

We usually baked this in individual seashells (15 minutes) and served them in the shells. For catering jobs, we would form thick patties and bake them for about 20 minutes.

SALMON CAKES

1 (15 ounce) can pink salmon

2 slices bread

1/2 teaspoon black pepper

1 tablespoon cider vinegar

Drain salmon and remove as many bones and as much of the black skin as possible. Crumble bread slices. Mix all ingredients together and form into patties. Fry over medium heat with a small amount of vegetable oil until well browned on both sides.

NOTE: Some people add an egg but my mother said eggs made the patties tough so we never used eggs.

MEETING STREET CRAB

This is a Charleston recipe. We served this in individual seashells.

Sauce: 4 tablespoons butter

4 tablespoons flour

1 cup heavy cream

1/4 teaspoon salt

1/8 teaspoon pepper

4 tablespoons white wine

Melt butter. Add flour and cook 1 minute, stirring constantly. Add salt, pepper, and cream and cook, stirring constantly, until very thick. Remove from heat. Stir in wine.

Mix 1/3 cup crab meat with 3 tablespoons sauce. Place in seashell. Sprinkle with 1-1/2 tablespoons grated cheddar cheese. Bake at 450° for 15 minutes until browning on top.

RED SNAPPER WITH ROASTED PECANS

1/2 teaspoon black pepper

1/2 teaspoon paprika

4 large red snapper filets

3 tablespoons butter

1/3 cup roasted pecans

1 tablespoon chopped fresh parsley

Lemon juice

Salt

Mix black pepper and paprika. Sprinkle on both sides of filets. Cook filets in 2 tablespoons butter over medium heat for 3-4 minutes on both sides.

Remove fish from pan and keep warm. Add remaining butter to pan and melt. Add pecans and cook 1 minute. Add lemon juice and salt. Pour over fish and sprinkle with parsley.

BOURBON GRILLED SALMON

4 Salmon filets

1 cup bourbon

1/2 cup brown sugar

1 clove garlic minced

2 tablespoon soy sauce

2 teaspoons fresh rosemary

1/4 cup olive oil

2 tablespoons lemon juice

Salt and pepper

Mix all ingredients except salmon in a bowl. Marinate salmon in this mixture for at least 30 minutes. Grill or sauté salmon over medium heat for 4 minutes on each side.

SHRIMP AND CHICKEN

1/2 cup butter

2 shallots, chopped (you may substitute scallions)

4-6 mushrooms, sliced

4 boneless chicken breasts, sliced

16 large shrimp

6 tablespoons brandy

6 tablespoons heavy cream

Salt & pepper to taste

Dried marjoram (or fresh chopped)

Sauté chicken breasts in butter until almost done. Add shallots and mushrooms and sauté for a couple of minutes. Add shrimp and continue to sauté until shrimp are done. Pour brandy over and flambé. Stir while the flame is dying down. Sprinkle all over with the marjoram. Add the cream, salt and pepper. Remove the chicken and shrimp and keep warm. Continue to cook the sauce over low heat until it is reduced and creamy. Pour over the chicken and shrimp and serve.

VEGETABLE LASAGNA

2 medium zucchini

1 small onion

1/2 medium green pepper

1 small carrot

1 stalk celery

1 small clove garlic

2 Tablespoons olive oil

23 oz. Diced canned tomatoes

1/4 cup red wine

1-1/2 Tablespoons dried parsley

1/2 teaspoon dried oregano

1/2 teaspoon dried thyme

1/2 teaspoon dried basil

1/4 teaspoon salt

1/4 teaspoon pepper

Uncooked lasagna noodles

6 oz. Ricotta cheese

8 oz. Shredded Swiss cheese

4 oz. Grated Parmesan cheese

1/2 cup water

Grate all vegetables or shred in a food processor. Mix first 15 ingredients in a large pot. Cover and bring to a boil; reduce heat and simmer 30 minutes. Uncover and simmer an additional 30 minutes, stirring occasionally.

In a lasagna pan, layer as follows:

A little sauce

Uncooked noodles

1/2 Ricotta cheese

1/2 Swiss cheese

1/2 Remaining sauce

Uncooked noodles

Remaining Ricotta cheese

Remaining Swiss cheese

Remaining sauce

Sprinkle with Parmesan cheese

Pour 1/2 cup water around edges

Bake at 350 for approximately 30 minutes until hot and bubbly and beginning to brown.

BASIC QUICHE

4 eggs

2 cups half & half

3/4 teaspoon salt

1/8 teaspoon pepper

Approximately 1-1/2 to 2 cups shredded Swiss cheese

1 unbaked 10 inch pie crust

Beat eggs very well until light and fluffy. Add half & half. Sprinkle cheese in pie crust. Pour egg mixture over. Sprinkle salt and pepper on top. Bake at 425° for 15 minutes; reduce heat and bake at 300° for 30 minutes.

FOR BROCCOLI-SWISS QUICHE

Sauté in butter enough broccoli flowerets to cover the bottom of the pie crust. Sauté approximately 2-3 tablespoons chopped onion. Sprinkle over broccoli. Sprinkle heavily with shredded Swiss cheese (at least 1 cup). Pour basic mixture over and bake as above.

FOR QUICHE LORRAINE

Chop 2 ounces ham and sprinkle in bottom of pie crust. Cook and crumble 6-8 slices of bacon. Sprinkle over ham. Sprinkle heavily with shredded Swiss cheese (at least 1 cup). Pour basic mixture over and bake as above.

ALFREDO SAUCE

We served alfredo sauce on cheese tortellini. This was a recipe I developed.

Melt 6 tablespoons butter. Add 4 tablespoons all-purpose flour.

Stir with a whisk until smooth over low heat.

Add 4 cups milk, 1 teaspoon salt, and ½ teaspoon pepper.

Cook over low heat, stirring constantly until it begins to thicken.

Stir in ½ cup (packed) shredded Parmesan cheese.

CAJUN SHRIMP SAUCE

Another popular dish was Cajun Shrimp. Mark Carroll developed this recipe. We made the sauce as the sauce above EXCEPT instead of Parmesan cheese, we

Added 1 tablespoon oregano and 1 tablespoon Cajun seasoning.

To prepare the shrimp, simply sauté the shrimp in butter until pink, add the sauce, and

Cook about 1 minute. Serve over angel hair pasta.

LIME FONDUE SAUCE

1 tablespoon cornstarch

1/2 cup cold water

4 tablespoons butter, cut into pieces

3 tablespoons Roses Lime Juice

Mix cornstarch and water (you must use cold water or the corn starch will glob up). Place in a double boiler over boiling water and cook, stirring constantly, until thickened. Add butter and lime juice. Stir until butter is melted.

NOTE: This sauce is delicious served over any kind of white fish. You may substitute lemon juice for the lime juice and have Lemon Fondue Sauce!

Cakes

ROSEMARY CAKE

1 stick butter softened

1/2 cup vegetable oil

1-3/4 cups sugar, divided

5 eggs, separated

2 teaspoons chopped fresh rosemary

Zest and juice of 1 lemon

1 cup buttermilk

1 teaspoon baking soda

2 cups all-purpose flour

1 teaspoon vanilla

1 cup shredded coconut

1/2 cup chopped pecans

Cream butter, oil and all but 2 tablespoons sugar until light and fluffy. Add egg yolks one at a time, beating well after each addition. Add chopped rosemary, lemon zest and juice.

Stir baking soda into buttermilk and let stand for a few minutes. Add flour and buttermilk into mixture alternately beginning and ending with flour. Stir in vanilla, coconut, and chopped pecans.

In a clean bowl, beat egg whites until soft peaks form, add 2 tablespoons sugar, and continue beating until stiff but not dry. Gently fold egg whites into the batter.

Pour into 3 greased and floured 9-inch pans and bake at 325° for approximately 20-25 minutes until cake springs back when touched and is beginning to pull away from edges of pan. Cool about 10 minutes, remove from pan, and cool completely before frosting.

ROSEMARY FROSTING

8 oz. Cream cheese softened

1 stick butter softened

1 teaspoon vanilla

2 teaspoons chopped fresh rosemary

Zest from 1 lemon

1 pound powdered sugar

1/2 cup chopped pecans

Beat cream cheese and butter until light and fluffy. Gradually add powdered sugar and beat until light and fluffy. Add vanilla, chopped rosemary, and chopped pecans.

NOTE: Wash sprigs of fresh rosemary under running water and wrap in paper towel to dry. Use kitchen shears to cut from stem. Chop with knife.

This cake freezes beautifully.

POUND CAKE

Originally, a pound cake was so named because it had a pound of sugar, a pound of flour, a pound of butter, and a pound of eggs. This is as true as you can get to that model.

1 pound butter (I sometimes use 1/2 pound butter and 1/2 pound margarine

4 scant cups sugar

10 eggs

4 full cups flour

2 teaspoons vanilla

2 teaspoons lemon flavoring

1 teaspoon almond flavoring

Cream butter and sugar until very light and fluffy. Add eggs one at a time, beating very well after each addition. Add flavorings and beat well. Gradually add flour and beat only until combined. Pour into greased and floured tube pan and bake at 300-325° for and hour and 15 minutes or until tests done with a cake tester.

NOTE: I usually start it at 325° and turn it down after an hour or so in order to keep it from getting too brown. You can successfully cut the recipe in half. You can freeze it.

CHOCOLATE POUND CAKE

1/2 pound butter

1/2 cup solid shortening (like Crisco)

3 cups sugar

5 eggs

1 teaspoon vanilla

3 cups flour

1/2 teaspoon baking powder

1/2 teaspoon salt

1/2 cup baking cocoa

1 cup milk

Cream together butter, shortening, and sugar. Add eggs one at a time beating well after each addition. Add vanilla. Sift together flour, baking power, salt, and cocoa and add alternately to batter with milk. Pour into greased and floured tube pan and bake at 325° for an hour and 20 minutes approximately until cake tester comes out clean. Let cool for about 15-20 minutes. Remove from pan and immediately wrap in plastic wrap. Let cool completely before frosting. This cake is delicious as is but fantastic if you frost it with Mother's Chocolate Fudge Frosting below!

MOTHER'S CHOCOLATE FUDGE FROSTING

4 oz. Unsweetened baking chocolate

1 pound powdered sugar

1 teaspoon vanilla

milk

Melt butter and chocolate over very low heat. Transfer to mixer bowl. Gradually add powdered sugar and enough (? 5-6 table-spoons or a little more or less!) milk, beating until spreading con-sistency. Add vanilla. This makes enough frosting to generously frost your pound cake. You can also use this frosting for a layer cake. It will make enough for 3 layers.

GERMAN CHOCOLATE CAKE

1 cup margarine

2-1/2 cups flour

2 cups sugar

4 eggs, separated

1 teaspoon baking soda dissolved in 1 cup buttermilk

One 8 oz. Package German Sweet Chocolate
  dissolved in 1/2 cup boiling water

1/4 teaspoon salt

Cream margarine and sugar until light and fluffy. Add egg yolks, beating well. Add flour alternately with milk. Add chocolate. Beat egg whites with salt until stiff but not dry. Gently fold egg whites into batter. Pour into 3 greased and floured cake pans and bake at 350 25-30 minutes until tester comes out clean. Cool for 10 minutes, remove from pans, and cool completely before frosting.

Time Changes: stories and recipes from *jovi's* kitchen

GERMAN CHOCOLATE FROSTING

2 cups sugar

1 15 oz. Can evaporated milk

1 cup chopped pecans

1 cup shredded coconut

3 egg yolks

1 stick butter

1 teaspoon vanilla

Put all ingredients in a saucepan, bring to boil, and cook slowly until thickened, about 20 minutes. Stir constantly. To test for doneness, put 3-4 drops on a saucer, turn sideways. If it doesn't run, then it is ready. Remove from heat, let cool. When cool, frost cake. We always frost between layers and around sides. Some people just put the frosting between the layers which is a lot easier but I don't think it looks as good!

HOT MILK CAKE

1/2 cup margarine or butter

1 cup milk

2 cups sugar

4 eggs

1 teaspoon baking powder

2 cups flour

1 teaspoon vanilla

Combine sugar and eggs and beat very well until light and fluffy. Add flour and baking powder. Add vanilla and beat well. Place butter and milk in saucepan and allow milk to slowly come to a boil or get hot enough to melt the butter. Pour into the batter and stir with your spatula until blended. DO NOT BEAT. Pour into 2 greased and floured cake pans and bake at 350 for approximately 25 minutes.

NOTE: Use this cake whenever you need white layers. It is delicious and easy. You can double the recipe for 4 layers and do 1-1/2 for 3 layers.

CARROT CAKE

2 cups all-purpose flour

2 teaspoons baking powder

1-1/2 teaspoons baking soda

1 teaspoon salt

2 teaspoons ground cinnamon

4 eggs

2 cups sugar

1-1/2 cups vegetable oil

2 cups (tightly packed) or 12 oz. Grated carrots

1 (8-1/2 oz.) can crushed pineapple, drained very well

1/2 cup chopped English walnuts

Sift together the flour, baking powder, baking soda, salt, and cinnamon. Beat eggs very well. Add sugar and oil until well combined. Stir in the flour. Mix carrots, walnuts, and pineapple with a little extra flour and fold into batter. Mix well. Pour into 3 greased and floured pans and bake at 350° for 35-40 minutes until cakes start to shrink from edges of pan. Cool in pans for 10 minutes or so. Remove from pans and cool completely before frosting.

CARROT CAKE FROSTING

1 stick butter softened

8 oz. Package Cream cheese softened

1 pound powdered sugar

1 teaspoon vanilla

Beat butter and Cream cheese until very light and fluffy. Add vanilla. Gradually add sugar, beating until combined.

CHOCOLATE LAYER CAKE

1-3/4 cups all-purpose flour

1 scant cup baking cocoa

1-1/4 teaspoon baking soda

1/8 teaspoon salt

3/4 cup (1-1/2 sticks) butter softened

2/3 cup granulated sugar

2/3 cup light brown sugar firmly packed

2 large eggs

2 teaspoons vanilla

1-1/2 cups buttermilk

Mix flour, cocoa, baking soda, and salt and set aside. Beat butter, granulated sugar and brown sugar until light and fluffy. Add eggs 1 at a time beating well after each addition. Add vanilla. At low speed, add flour mixture and milk alternately, beating just until blended. Pour into 2 greased and floured pans and bake at 350° for approximately 25-30 minutes until tester comes out clean. Cool in pans for 10 minutes. Remove from pans and cool completely before frosting.

NOTE: You can frost with the Chocolate Fudge Frosting or Chocolate Buttercream Frosting.

SHAKER CAKE

This recipe is an adaptation of Mother Ann's Birthday Cake which was an old Shaker recipe. I always told our guests that the big difference was that the Shaker's stirred the batter with a peach tree branch and I did not do that!

1 cooked layer of Hot Milk Cake

Peach preserves

Split layer in half and spread bottom half with peach preserves and replace top half.

Frost with almond flavored whipped cream below. Refrigerate for several hours or overnight.

FROSTING

1-1/4 cup whipping cream

1-1/2 tablespoons powdered sugar

1-1/2 teaspoon almond extract

1/3 cup sliced almonds, toasted

Whip cream until starts to thicken. Add powdered sugar and almond extract. Continue whipping until stiff. Spread over top and sides of cake.

Sprinkle almonds over top just before serving.

NEW YORK STYLE CHEESECAKE

5 (8 ounce) packages cream cheese softened

1-1/2 cups sugar

3 eggs

2-1/2 teaspoons vanilla

Graham cracker crust

Mix 1-2/3 cups graham cracker crumbs and 1/3 cup melted butter. Press into 10-inch springform pan and set aside.

Beat cream cheese at high speed until light and fluffy. Gradually add sugar, beating well. Add eggs, one at a time, beating well after each addition. Stir in vanilla. Pour into prepared crust. Bake at 350 for 40 minutes. Turn oven off and prop oven door open part way. Leave cheesecake in oven for 30 minutes. Remove from oven and let cool on a rack. Cover and chill for at least 8 hours.

We used this same recipe for Chocolate Cheesecake by simply adding 12 ounces of melted chocolate chips to the batter at the end and substituting 1/2 teaspoon almond extract for the vanilla. To make a chocolate crumb crust, mix 2 cups crushed Oreo cookies and 2-3 tablespoons melted butter.

BLACK STRAWBERRY CAKE

My daughter Wendy told me about a cake she had eaten in Atlanta and I came up with the following version. It was a pain to make and we didn't have it very often but people loved it. I used 2 cooked layers of the Chocolate Layer Cake recipe.

TO ASSEMBLE:

1. Brush (to clean) enough strawberries to cover the top of the cake layer. It is easier if you use small berries for this.

2. Melt 3/4 cup chocolate chips and about 2 tablespoons margarine over very low heat.

3. Dip strawberries in chocolate and lay on waxed paper to set. Put strawberries in refrigerator to firm up.

4. Whip 1 cup whipping cream with 3 tablespoons powdered sugar and 1 teaspoon vanilla. This should be firm.

5. Spread 1/2 the whipped cream on one cake layer leaving 1/4 inch around edge.

6. Place strawberries tightly all over the whipped cream.

7. Spread remainder of whipped cream over the top of strawberries.

8. Place second cake layer on top. Put cake in refrigerator while preparing ganache.

9. Break up 6 oz. Swiss bittersweet chocolate in bowl. Heat a little more than 1/2 cup heavy cream just to boiling point. Pour over chocolate; let sit for a few minutes. Stir until smooth.

10. Pour/spread/drizzle over top of cake. Keep cake refrigerated.

11. Serve with strawberry sauce. Mash a few fresh strawberries and add a little sugar and a little cornstarch. Cook until it just begins to thicken. Cool and refrigerate until ready to serve.

BROWNSTONE FRONT CAKE

This was another recipe Lisa McCamy suggested we make. It is very good.

1/2 cup water

2 oz. Unsweetened baking chocolate

1 teaspoon baking soda

1 cup (2 sticks) butter softened

2 cups sugar

3 large eggs

3 cups all-purpose flour

1 cups buttermilk

1 teaspoon vanilla

In a small saucepan, heat the water until it begins to steam. Remove from heat, add the chocolate and baking soda. Cover and let stand for 5 minutes. Cool to room temperature.

Cream butter and sugar until light and fluffy. Add eggs one at a time beating well after each addition. Beat in the cooled chocolate mixture. Add the flour and buttermilk alternately until well incorporated. Beat in the vanilla and continue to beat, scraping down the sides of bowl, until the batter is a uniform color. Pour into 3 greased and floured pans and bake at 350° for 25-30 minutes until tester comes out clean. Cool in pans 10 minutes. Remove from pans and cool completely before frosting. Frost with Caramel Frosting.

CARAMEL FROSTING

2/3 cup butter

1 cup firmly packed light brown sugar

1/2 cup milk

1 pound powdered sugar

1 teaspoon vanilla

Melt butter in saucepan. Add brown sugar and milk and heat to boiling, stirring constantly. Boil gently for 5 minutes. Remove from heat and cool for 10 minutes. Blend in powdered sugar, beating until smooth. Add vanilla.

CARAMEL CAKE

Our Caramel Cake was a favorite with many people. We used the Hot Milk Cake recipe and frosted it with the Caramel Frosting. Sometime we would sprinkle chopped pecans on top.

CHOCOLATE FINESSE CAKE

This is a recipe I developed myself. I asked Pansy Sullivan to name it for me. She wrote me a four-page response giving all of her thought process in coming up with a name! Anyone who remembers Pansy will understand this! She came up with Chocolate Finesse and I think it was a great name.

2 cooked layers of Chocolate Layer Cake

Between layers spread the following filling:

16 ounces ricotta cheese

1/4 cup sugar

2 tablespoons dark rum

1/4 teaspoon salt

1/3 cup chopped chocolate chips

1/3 cup chopped pecans

Beat ricotta cheese, sugar, rum, and salt until smooth. (You can do this with the mixer or the food processor) Stir in nuts and choco- late. Frost cake with Chocolate Buttercream Frosting

BUTTER CREAM FROSTING

This is real buttercream frosting, not the shortening kind that most bakeries use!

VANILLA BUTTERCREAM FROSTING

1 cup butter softened

1 teaspoon vanilla

1 pound powdered sugar

2 tablespoons milk

Cream butter until light and fluffy. Add vanilla. Gradually add sugar beating well. Scrape down sides of bowl. Add milk and beat at high speed until light and fluffy.

CHOCOLATE BUTTERCREAM
Add 1 cup sifted baking cocoa and 1-2 tablespoons more milk.

LEMON BUTTERCREAM
Add zest and juice from one lemon and omit milk.

WALNUT CAKE WITH CHOCOLATE WHIPPED CREAM FROSTING

2 cups walnut pieces

2 tablespoons all-purpose flour

6 large eggs, separated

1/4 teaspoon salt

1 cup sugar

1 teaspoon vanilla

1/4 teaspoon cream of tartar

Grease three 8 inch cake pans. Line the bottoms with parchment paper or waxed paper. Grease the paper.

Place the nuts, flour, and salt in food processor and process with steel blade until finely ground. Set aside.

Beat the egg yolks with the sugar until the mixture lightens in color and thickens. Add the vanilla and beat until well combined. Mix in the nut mixture by hand until well combined. The batter will be very thick. Set aside.

In a clean bowl, beat the egg whites with the cream of tartar until stiff but not dry. Fold a third of the whites into the egg/nut mixture, incorporating thoroughly. Fold in the remaining whites gently, until well combined.

Pour into the prepared pans and bake at 350 for 30-35 minutes until each layer springs back when touched lightly in the center. Cool for 10 minutes. Remove from pan and cool completely before frosting.

CHOCOLATE WHIPPED CREAM FROSTING

4 ounces semisweet chocolate (you can use chocolate chips)

2 cups heavy cream

1 teaspoon vanilla

1/2 cup chopped walnuts

In the top of double boiler set over simmering water, melt the chocolate with 1/2 cup of the cream. Stir until chocolate is completely melted and the mixture is smooth. Cool to room temperature. Beat the remainder of the cream until it begins to thicken. Add the chocolate and vanilla and continue to beat until mixture forms soft peaks. Spread topping between layers and on sides. Sprinkle with walnuts.

LEMON CAKE

Cake: 2 cooked layers of Hot Milk Cake

Filling: Lemon Curd (recipe below)

Frosting: Lemon Buttercream Frosting

Lemon Curd Ingredients:

2 cups sugar

1-1/2 teaspoons lemon zest

1/2 cup lemon juice

1 cup butter

4 eggs, beaten

Combine first four ingredients in top of double boiler; bring water to a boil. Reduce heat to low, and cook until butter melts, stirring constantly. Gradually stir about one-fourth of the hot mixture into the eggs, stirring constantly. Add warmed eggs to remaining hot mixture, stirring constantly. Cook in top of double boiler, stirring constantly, for 20 minutes or until thickened. Remove from heat and allow to cool. Chill for 2 hours.

NOTE: This will make more than you need for the cake but it will keep a long time in the freezer and it is delicious used in many other ways.

Assembly: Place one layer of cake on plate. Spread a thick layer of curd over cake leaving about 1/2 inch around edge. Place second layer on top. Frost with Lemon Buttercream Frosting. Keep refrigerated.

FIG CAKE

When we had fresh figs available, I would make this occasionally. You can also use fig preserves, but they are so good on a hot biscuit, why mess them up!

- 2 cups all purpose flour
- 1-1/2 cups sugar
- 1 teaspoon salt
- 1 teaspoon baking soda
- 1 teaspoon each: ground cloves, ground nutmeg, ground cinnamon
- 3 large eggs, lightly beaten
- 1 cup vegetable oil
- 1 cup buttermilk
- 1 teaspoon vanilla
- 1 cup (packed) chopped fresh figs or fig preserves
- 1/2 cup chopped pecans (optional)

Stir together first 7 ingredients. Stir in egg, oil, and buttermilk, blending well. Stir in vanilla. Fold in figs and pecans. Pour into a greased and floured 13x9 inch pan and bake at 325° for 35 minutes or until a tester comes out clean. Pierce top of cake several times with a wooden toothpick and drizzle Buttermilk Glaze over top. Cool.

BUTTERMILK GLAZE

- 1 cup sugar
- 1/2 cup butter
- 1/2 cup buttermilk
- 1 tablespoon light corn syrup

1 teaspoon vanilla

Bring all ingredients to a boil and cook 3 minutes.

NOTE: I usually made this in two loaf pans instead of one large pan. That way you can freeze one of them!

Pies

CHOCOLATE CHESS PIE

8 (1 stick) tablespoons butter

2 squares unsweetened baking chocolate

1 cup sugar

2 eggs beaten

1-1/2 teaspoon vanilla

Dash salt

1 unbaked 8 or 9 inch pie crust

Melt butter and chocolate on very low heat or top of double boiler. Beat eggs very well with a wire whisk. Add sugar, salt, and vanilla. Add chocolate mixture and stir until well blended. Pour into pie crust and bake at 350° for30-35 minutes until set. Cool.

DERBY PIE

2 eggs

1 cup sugar

1/2 cup all purpose flour

1/2 cup melted butter

1 teaspoon vanilla

1 cup mini chocolate chips

1 cup chopped walnuts

1 unbaked 8 or 9 inch pie crust

Beat eggs very well with wire whisk. Stir in sugar and flour. Add butter and vanilla. Stir until blended. Stir in chocolate chips and walnuts. Pour into pie crust and bake at 350° for approximately 45 minutes or until set.

jovi's LEMON PIE

4 eggs

1 lemon

1 stick margarine or butter

2 cups sugar

In blender or food processor, blend eggs until light. Add lemon which has been sliced very thin and seeds removed. Blend until smooth. Add margarine and blend. Add sugar and blend again until VERY smooth. Pour into pie crust and bake at 350° for 40-50 minutes until set.

BLACKBERRY COBBLER

Blackberries (fresh or frozen)

Sugar

Flour

Butter

Pie Crust

Place berries in pan. Mix sugar and flour and sprinkle over berries. Cut butter in small pieces and scatter over berries. Cover with pie crust. Bake at 400° until crust is golden brown. Note: you can brush the top of the crust with egg/water mixture before baking.

I didn't give quantities because you should make whatever size you need so that it all gets eaten right away! Don't make it too sweet because you probably want to serve vanilla ice cream with it! I think about ¾ cup of sugar for a quart of berries is about right with about 2 tablespoons of flour. If you have more or less berries, you can adjust the quantity of sugar and flour based on this. Frozen pie crust works great unless you really want to make your own!

PECAN PIE

2 tablespoons butter softened

1 cup light brown sugar, packed

2 tablespoons all purpose flour

1 cup light corn syrup

3 eggs

1 cup chopped pecans

1 teaspoon vanilla

3/4 teaspoon salt

1 unbaked 8 or 9 inch pie crust

Beat eggs with wire whisk very well. Add sugar and flour. Add corn syrup, eggs, vanilla, and salt. Blend well. Stir in pecans. Pour into pie crust and bake at 350 for 40 to 45 minutes until set.

GRASSHOPPER PIE

CRUST: 1 cup chocolate wafer crumbs

1 tablespoon sugar

3 tablespoons butter

Mix all together and press into bottom and sides of 8 or 9 inch pie plate. Bake at 350° for 5 to 7 minutes. Cool.

FILLINGS:

24 large marshmallows

1/4 cup milk

2 tablespoons white crème de cacao

3 tablespoons green crème de menthe

1 cup heavy cream, whipped

In top of double boiler, melt marshmallows in milk. Set aside to cool completely.

When cool, add crème de cacao and crème de menthe. Fold marshmallow mixture into the whipped cream. Pour into cooled crust. Place in freezer. When frozen, wrap with plastic wrap and aluminum foil. Serve directly from freezer. Garnish with whipped cream is desired.

NOTE: Will keep in freezer for several weeks.

COCONUT CUSTARD PIE

2 eggs

1 tablespoon all purpose flour

1 cup sugar

1/2 cup milk

1/4 cup butter, melted

1-1/2 teaspoons vanilla

6 ounces shredded coconut

1 unbaked 8 or 9 inch pie crust

Beat eggs very well with wire whisk. Add all other ingredients and pour into pie crust. Bake at 350° until set, about 35 to 40 minutes.

CHOCOLATE ANGEL PIE

Meringue Crust:
2 egg whites
1/2 cup sugar

1 teaspoon vanilla

1/2 cup finely chopped pecans

Beat egg whites until foamy. Gradually add sugar, beating until very stiff. Fold in vanilla and pecans. Spread in greased 8 or 9 inch pie plate. Bake at 300° approximately one hour until lightly browned and dry. Remove from heat and cool completely.

Filling:

1 cup semi-sweet chocolate chips

5 tablespoons water

1-1/4 cups heavy cream

Melt chocolate in water over very low heat. Set aside to cool. Whip cream until stiff. Fold chocolate into cream. Spread into crust and refrigerate. Keeps just a couple of days.

NOTE: You can make the crust a couple of days ahead. Place in airtight container or wrap very well. We used to make bite-size meringues just a spoonful at a time with a slight indentation on a greased cookie sheet. Bake about 20 minutes. They will keep several days if you keep them airtight. Fill with the chocolate mousse recipe above or use the Lemon Curd recipe. Makes delicious bite-size sweets for a party!

MACAROON TART SHELLS

2 cups flaked sweetened coconut

1/2 cup sugar

1/4 cup plus 2 tablespoons all purpose flour

1 teaspoon vanilla

2 egg whites

Vegetable cooking spray

Combine first 5 ingredients in a bowl, blending well. Spray muffin pans (1 dozen cup size) with vegetable cooking spray. Spoon mixture into pans, pressing into bottom and up sides of cups. Bake at 400° for 15 minutes or until edges are just beginning to brown. DO NOT OVERBAKE. Cool 2 minutes, then remove from pans and cool completely.

Fill tart shells with Lemon Curd and garnish with whipped cream, if desired.

EGG CUSTARD PIE

¼ cup butter, softened

2/3 cup sugar

2 eggs

3 tablespoons all purpose flour

¾ cup evaporated milk

¼ cup water

1 teaspoon vanilla

1 unbaked 9-inch pie crust

Cream butter and sugar very well. Add eggs, one at a time, beating well after each addition. Add flour and mix thoroughly. Stir in milk, water, and vanilla. Pour into pie crust and bake at 400° for 20 minutes. Reduce heat and bake at 300° for 15 minutes or until firm. Cool. Refrigerate until thoroughly chilled.

Other Sweets

SUGAR COOKIES

1/2 cup butter

1 cup sugar

1 large egg

2 cups all purpose flour

1 teaspoon baking powder

1/2 teaspoon salt

1/2 teaspoon vanilla

Cream butter and sugar very well. Blend in egg. Sift dry ingredients and add to mixture. Add vanilla. Divide dough in half and roll, one part at a time, to 1/8 inch thickness. Cut with cookie cutters into desired shape. Transfer to cookie sheet and bake at 375° for 8 to 10 minutes.

GINGER SNAPS

1-1/2 cups margarine

2 cups light brown sugar, firmly packed

2 large eggs

1/2 cup molasses

4 cups all purpose flour

1/2 teaspoon salt

4 teaspoons baking soda

2 teaspoons ground cloves

2 teaspoons ground ginger

2 teaspoons ground cinnamon

Sugar

Combine all ingredients except Sugar. Form into small balls. Roll balls of dough in sugar. Bake at 350° approximately 10 minutes.

SHORTBREAD

1 cup butter

1/2 cup sugar

2-1/2 cups all purpose flour

Combine butter and sugar until well blended. Stir in flour. Chill dough several hours or overnight. On lightly floured surface, roll out dough to 1/4 inch thickness. Cut into desired shapes. You may also press dough into shortbread molds or press into round pan.

If you press into pan, mark the cuts prior to baking so you can cut it without breaking.

Bake at 300° until lightly browned. Time depends on size of cookies.

NOTE: You may add raisins, dried cranberries, dried cherries, or chopped fresh rosemary for different flavors.

NUT SANDIES

1/2 cup butter

1/2 cup margarine

3/4 cup sugar

1 tablespoon distilled white vinegar

1-3/4 cup flour

1/2 teaspoon baking soda

1 cup finely chopped pecans OR walnuts

Cream butter and margarine. Add sugar and vinegar and beat until fluffy. Sift flour and soda and add to mixture. Stir in nuts. Drop by teaspoonful onto ungreased baking sheets. Bake for 30 minutes at 300°.

DOUBLE CHOCOLATE BROWNIES

1 cup butter, plus extra for pan

12 ounces unsweetened baking chocolate

8 large eggs

4 cups sugar

2 teaspoons vanilla

2-1/2 cups all purpose flour

2-1/2 teaspoons baking powder

1 teaspoon salt

2 cups chopped walnuts

Melt chocolate and butter in saucepan over very low heat. Cool for 5 minutes. In a large bowl, beat eggs with whisk until fluffy. Add sugar and vanilla, blending well. Add the chocolate and butter. Mix well. Add the flour, baking powder and salt and mix well. Stir in the walnuts. Spread the batter into a pan that has been well greased with butter. Bake 30 minutes. Do not overcook. Cool completely before cutting.

ALMOND CRESCENTS

1 cup butter

1/2 cup sugar

2 tablespoons water

2 cups all purpose flour

1 cup chopped almonds

1 teaspoon almond flavoring

Powdered sugar

Cream butter and sugar until fluffy. Add water, flour, flavorings, and almonds. Mix thoroughly. Shape into small crescents. Bake on ungreased cookie sheet at 350 for 15 minutes. Cool slightly and then roll in powdered sugar.

BERRIED TREASURE

This was a favorite dessert at jovi's. We usually filled a dish with sliced fresh strawberries, spooned on the topping, and sprinkled with a little brown sugar. You can also use blueberries, raspberries, peaches, or some combination of them.

TOPPING:

6 ounces cream cheese, softened

8 ounces sour cream

1/3 cup light brown sugar, packed

Beat cream cheese until smooth. Add sour cream and brown sugar and beat until smooth. Chill.

PRALINE SUNDAE SAUCE

1-1/2 cup light brown sugar

2/3 cup light corn syrup

4 tablespoons butter

1 small can evaporated milk

Mix the first 3 ingredients and heat to boiling point. Remove from stove and cool. When lukewarm, add milk. Blend well. Store in jar in refrigerator. Delicious on ice cream or cheesecake. Keeps a long time.

FRESH ORANGE SORBET

2-1/2 cups water

1 cup sugar

Orange rind strips from 2 oranges

2-2/3 cups fresh orange juice

1/3 cup fresh lemon juice

Combine water and sugar in small saucepan and bring to a boil. Add orange strips and reduce heat. Simmer for about 5 minutes. Discard strips and let liquid cool completely.

Add orange juice and lemon juice. Pour mixture into a container and freeze.

CRANBERRY SORBET

3 cups pureed cranberries

3 cups water

1-1/2 cups sugar

1 tablespoon lemon juice

Mix all together and freeze until slushy. Beat with a mixer for 2 minutes. Freeze completely.

LEMON SORBET

2 cups water

1 cup sugar

1 tablespoon grated lemon rind

1 cup lemon juice

Mix all together. Freeze, scraping occasionally until completely frozen.

About the Authors

Sisters Jonnie Anderson and Vivian Jones left their cushy corporate jobs and threw open the doors of *jovi's cafe* on Jones Street in Historic Wake Forest North Carolina in 1991. The restaurant was a big hit with locals and visitors alike.

The pair reside in a loft in downtown Wake Forest where Vivian is the first female mayor of Wake Forest. Jonnie is active in the Wake Forest Chamber of Commerce and the Downtown Revitalization Corporation. She also travels weekly to her hometown to spend time with their aging father.

Notes

Printed in the United States
127402LV00001B/11-166/P

9 780977 315680